THE ENGLISH DRAGON BOOK 4

KATHI S. BARTON

World Castle Publishing, LLC
Pensacola, Florida
Copyright © Kathi S. Barton 2018
Paperback ISBN: 9781629899176
eBook ISBN: 9781629899183
First Edition World Castle Publishing, LLC, April 2, 2018
http://www.worldcastlepublishing.com
Licensing Notes
Cover: Karen Fuller
Editor: Maxine Bringenberg

Table of Contents

Chapter 1

Em was exhausted, but more than that, she was terrified as well. To be in the house of the king was unnerving, but the way that everyone kept coming in to check on her was also making her afraid. Like instead of checking on her, they were making sure that she wasn't harming the household and the people there. She looked at Sebastian when he growled low.

"What is it?" Someone comes, he told her. "Well, that's not at all helpful. People have been coming in and out all day long. It would be easier for you to say that no one is out there."

The door opened and a man she'd not met before stood there. He didn't enter the room, but he did watch her. Asking him what his deal was, he told her nothing but continued to wait. Sitting up in the bed cost her, but she thought it was worth it to have him go away. Which he did not.

"My name is Dana Blankenship. You are an emerald dragon, fittingly called Emerald." She nodded. "Your gryphon is called Sebastian and he is not one to mess with. He's been caring for you for many decades. You ask yourself

5

why I know this. Well, the household has spoken of nothing else but the beautiful woman who is an emerald dragon. Oh, and her sidekick, Sebastian."

He was very handsome. His face was hard, but she knew that when he smiled, like he was right now, he could not just open doors, but women would swoon and men would be jealous. He was a man that people paid attention to. She was not going to be charmed by him though.

"Yes, so what? You know what everyone in the house does, big deal." He nodded, then shook his head. "You're getting on my last nerve, and if you knew anything about me, you'd know that I don't care for that."

"You're the queen of the emeralds. That part I figured out all on my own." Her heart began pounding in her chest and she thought about what she needed to do now. "You make all the emeralds in the world. Meaning that all you can make, cry, is the same gem. Your job is to make sure that there are just enough and not too many in one place. Correct?"

Terror made her snappish. Well, more snappish than she normally would be. And while she rarely held back when she was mad, this time it got away from her even before she opened her mouth.

"What the fuck are you doing? Reciting my entire life's history? What are you doing here anyway?" He asked if he could come into her room. "Not yet. I think I like you better right where you are. And I want to know, what it is you think you know that I don't?"

"I'm sure that I know a great deal, but not necessarily more than you. You're the sister of the opal, ruby, and sapphire. I'm assuming that since you're Emerald, their names are accordingly." She told him that was right. "Are the others

6

safe?"

"Why would you even care? I don't know you from anyone." He just nodded and leaned against the door jamb like he had not a care in the world. "What are you? Other than a dragon. You must have some kind of special powers. Otherwise you wouldn't have been able to figure this all out."

"What I have is a tenacious sister-in-law that has read over the rules and regulations of our kind. Which would include you and your family. Quinn is the one to see if you have any questions about any kind of dragon. And she's reading the books that are a part of the council as well. Smart girl, that Quinn. And she has an equally smart sister. Her name is Carmine if you ever get the chance to meet her." She nodded, thinking that this could be really bad for the rest of them. She was in the house of someone that could hurt her worse than she was already. "I don't know what's going on in your head right now, but I'm not going to hurt you. None of you."

"And you think that I should just believe you? Not likely. I've been around longer than you have." He said that she hadn't, actually. "That's...I can't smell you."

"No, you cannot. Where are the others, Em? Are they safe? I know that you travel together, wherever you go. Are they safe?" She didn't want to answer him, but the truth was, she didn't know if they were or not and told him that. "If you'd like, we can go and bring them here. This is a safe haven for dragons."

"You tell me why I can't smell you, then perhaps I'll trust you." He asked again if he could come into the room. "Why do you need my permission?"

"For the simple reason that you won't give it."

As she was growling low at him, he turned to his right

and smiled. It was a smile that made her heart flutter and her body warm. When he took a tray from the woman that had been in here earlier, she sat up higher in the bed when he brought the tray to her. His whispered breath touched her cheek.

"I'm a diamond dragon. You're not my mate as I had assumed. But one of your sisters, perhaps? The smell on you, it gives me only a hint of her, one of the other three. Which is it, I wonder? And what would a diamond dragon have with a gem one should they have children? All things that I plan to figure out. With or without your help." She shook her head, telling him in the same low voice that she wasn't going to help him. "All right then, Em. I'll see you later. And if you change your mind, let me know."

Change her mind about what? Then she remembered that he wanted to keep the others safe. In all this time she'd not reached out to her sisters, and looked at Sabastian to send him on his way to find them.

"Bring them back if you do find that they need me." He said that he could do that. "Sebastian, while you're with them, warn them where I am. The diamond dragon is tricky."

"My lady, if you don't mind my saying, I think you're tricky as well. But he knows a great deal. It might not harm you to be a little nicer to him." Em pointed out that he wasn't terribly nice to her. "Yes, but you put up your shield well before you knew what he was to one of your sisters."

After they left, both Sebastian and the dragon, Em thought about what had happened. The dragon had warmed her body. Not in a sexual way, but more like one would a relative, a brother so to speak. He had given her a hint of what he was. Yes, he'd told her he was a diamond dragon, but that

8

could have been nothing more than wishful thinking on his part. He had even told her his name, knew hers as well. But the thing was, he could have been lying.

I don't lie. His voice echoed through her mind like he was standing in the room with her. *You and I, we'll have to learn to trust each other. Because we both know that I'm going to be mated to one of your sisters. Which one, I haven't any idea, but we'll be related.*

How do you know that? He laughed, and it warmed her more than the small breath had. *I don't think I'd like to be related to you. You're not a nice person.*

Then we should get along splendidly.

His laughter made her think that he'd just insulted her. And Em didn't like it any more than she did the man.

As the day wore on and she was feeling better with all the fresh meat and vegetables, Em was even happy that someone had taken the time to know what she needed to eat. However, it was her leg that scared her the most. The man who had hit her with the iron, he had known what he was about.

She wasn't cut badly, but until all the iron was out, and there would be a great deal of it, she would get weaker until she was no more. Not die—she was too strong for that—but she'd not be able to produce tears, nor would she be able to help her sisters when necessary. Weakness was not an option when you were a gem dragon.

Your sisters are coming to you. They are terrified, if you wish the truth of it. I have told them of the man. They are both excited and afraid that he will not suit them. Em pointed out that they could hide out in the woods and meet him one at a time. After a brief pause, he told them that was what they were going to do. *They wish to know how you are faring today. I told them that*

9

you were getting stronger, but that someone will need to take the iron from your body. And that you're being most stubborn about it.

I'm not being stubborn, I'm being practical. And that is not going to get us all killed. She laid back on the bed and thought about what it would take for her to be healed completely. *I will need a great dragon to help me. And the king will not bother himself with a lesser dragon such as myself.*

And what, pray, do you think the world would do without your beautiful gems? She smiled at the tone of her sister, Sapphire, and had to laugh when she told her not to be a dimwit. They were forever picking up words to insult each other with. *Ask for help or you'll be gone.*

Em had met the king. But because of what she was, he'd not known about the iron. Now that she had time to think about it, she knew that then would have been the perfect time to ask for the help. But she'd been as stubborn as her sister had accused her of being. Things were not going well for her at the moment.

"Hello." She looked at the little girl standing at the foot of the bed, startled by her appearance. "I'm Carmine. My sister said that I could come and see you. But I'm not to bother you if you don't want me to."

"It's all right. I was just thinking. Do you live here?" She nodded. "I'm sure you can visit me any time you wish. My name is Em. I'm a dragon too."

"An emerald dragon. Uncle Dana told me that you're very special, and that we needed to never ever tell anyone that you're here. Otherwise they'll come for you, like they do me." That scared her too. Was there nothing normal about this family? "I can help you."

"Help me what?" Instead of answering, Carmine moved

to the side of the bed and pulled the blanket away, unwrapping the leaves that Em had wrapped around the wound. Em hissed when they stuck to the wound. "It's not that bad."

"It's terrible. The man who did this to you, he's on his way. He doesn't know where you are, but he does know that you're close to him. The wound there, it's going to keep festering until you're dead. Iron wouldn't normally kill you, but you're much too weak now. I would say if its not removed very soon, it'll hit your brain and kill you. As simple as that." She didn't want to believe her, but she knew that her words were true. "I really can help you. But you have to let me. Quinn said that its rude to assume that I'm smarter than everyone in the world."

"Are you?" The little girl seemed to think of her question when it had only been a joke. "Your name is Carmine, you said. Why are you so smart?"

"I have this brain thingy. My sister said that it's because my brain is so big. But the doctor, a vampire, he told me that I have a nudge in my brain. It makes me use most of my brain, a lot that most people don't. I use ninety-four percent while the average person uses ten percent. Some even less." She asked if the less were the handicapped. "No. Some of them use a great deal of their brain, more than a lot of smart people. But they have trouble with it because they don't know how to process it. They know what to do and how to do it, it's just harder for them because they don't know the names of things, such as a hammer. They might know pounding thing, but that's what gets them labeled as a handicapped person to begin with. Their lack of ability of what to call them."

"I see." She did too. "How are you able to fix my leg? And you're right, it is badly infected. I'm afraid of having to cut

11

my leg off."

"It's well past being in only your leg. It is racing over your body as we talk. But Dana is going to help me." She started to tell her that she didn't like the other man, but he was in the room before she could. "He's very strong and he can hold you down. I'm really sorry, but you're going to hurt like the dickens."

"Why would *he* need to hold me down? Isn't there anyone else? I mean, he must have things to do." But he got onto the bed with her and behind her. When she was wrapped in his arms, he handed her a small stone, a dark emerald. "I can crush this and eat it? How did you know...the sister-in-law?"

"Yes, but not until she's done, please?"

She said that she'd wait. Afraid of what was going to happen, she held onto him while he wrapped her into his arms. This was going to be painful, she knew that. The room filled with light and all her sisters were there.

~~~

Dana was careful not to breath too deeply. One of them, the Sisters of Four, was his mate. But now was not the time to try and figure that out. Emerald needed him. She was strong, and could hurt Carmine while she was in pain. And he knew that she was going to be in a great deal of it before this ended. Each of the women surrounded the bed, lending, he had no doubt, their magic to Carmine.

"I'm going to pull it free of you, but you're going to be really hurt. Like I said, it's all over you now." Em nodded in his arms. "It's all through your blood, and that's going to have to be collected too. Enough so that I can make the shard it came from. You understand me?"

"Yes. All right. But where is the king? He must be here in

12

the event I don't make it." Carmine told them all that he was coming. Ruby, dressed all in her color from head to toe, smiled as she continued. "He'll not be happy about this, I think."

"He'll be fine." Dana had already let him know what was going on. And that they were going to take out the iron. He'd been surprised to know that; he'd not smelled it on her at all.

"I mean, don't you think, being the dragon all mighty, that I should have smelled something?" His mom hit him on the head. "I was just joking, Mother. Honestly, how did we all miss that?"

"More than likely because she didn't want you to know." Danburn asked why she'd do that. "You're the king. She's a dragon. You add it up."

"She's afraid of me? Why? I'm a puppy." Kendrick snorted. "I am. I'm very nice, all the time. I mean, I have my moments, but everyone does."

"But not everyone rules, nor are they big enough to stomp on a house and kill everyone in it. Blend into the trees and woods surrounding him so that no one sees him. Oh, and let's not forget that you have teeth that are longer than most grown men, and they're as sharp as razors."

"Minor things when someone is seeking help." She snorted at him again and Dana had to laugh. "Darling, you should get that looked into. You seem to have a slight cold."

And now Danburn was there with them, lending whatever help was needed. Dana wondered in that moment why he'd taken so long to come and visit his friend. He was a great one too. The men here, probably the only true ones that he had.

"You have to help me a little at a time, please. Like one of you touch me when we go searching, and then when they're tired, the next one." She grinned at them all and Dana laughed.

13

This child was so young, yet had the soul of a very old person. "Okay, let's do this."

The first bit of iron came from the wound, and when it hovered just above Em's leg, Dana had no idea what was going on. He thought, wrongly so, that he was to reach for it. But when the second, then a third piece came from Em's flesh, he knew that Carmine was forming the shard to make sure that it was all there.

It took a lot longer than he thought it should have. Em had passed out from the pain. He'd never thought of how it would be removed from her body, but the fact that wherever it was it just came out of her skin startled him. There were bleeding marks all over her body that made him slightly ill. To him it looked like they had it all, but Carmine, who was covered in sweat, said there was one more.

Danburn had long since fallen to the side, as well as most of her sisters. Sapphire was still standing, lending her magic, as was Danielle, their vampire friend. Dana had started to move, since he was doing nothing more than sitting on the bed, when Sapphire told him to sit still.

Don't move. You're keeping her strength up. She might be passed out from the pain, but you're keeping her alive. He looked down at the bloodied woman. *She's going to need something fresh, with a great deal of red meat.*

I'll arrange that now. Sapphire nodded, but said nothing more while he asked Kendrick for help with it. *She'll make it. You know that, don't you?*

I know no such thing. Had I known she'd been hurt, we'd have taken care of it days ago. Not waiting until it was nearly too late. Her tone was nasty, much like Ruby's was. Opal was gentler than the other two. She wasn't without a temper, but she had a nicer way of getting her point across. *Just pay attention to what you're doing, and perhaps we can all be hopeful.*

He didn't have a clue what he was supposed to be doing that needed his undivided attention. The patient was out cold, and he was not supposed to move. Whatever, he thought. If Sapphire was his mate, someone was going to be in for a rude awakening. And he had a feeling that it was going to be him, he thought with a smile.

When the tiny piece was added to the shard, Carmine passed out too, just tumbling to the floor like a rag doll. Quinn came in to get her then, afraid to be in the room for too long while they were working for fear of her child. That was why Kendrick wasn't allowed to join in the help. The babes needed their mothers to be very strong.

Dana loved this family, and figured that when Hanson had found his mate, it was only a matter of time before him and the other two got theirs. Kip was biting at the bit for his mate, while Griffith was more sedate about it. He couldn't care less either way. Dana thought that it wasn't a front either — Griffith was really that laid back of a man and dragon. But he had a temper. Like the rest of them, their dragons would take them in no time if there was a problem. But he did notice that the men with mates, their dragons were different, treading lightly, literally, when the women were about.

He'd laughed his ass off the other night when all of them had ganged up on Griffith. He'd apparently trampled the flowers that were newly planted and had killed a prize rose bush. In less time than he thought it possible, not only was Griffith out there replanting the flowers, but he'd brought one of the roses from around his own castle, a very rare and old breed, to replace the one that he'd killed. Everyone was

15

happy after that, and Griffith and the rest of them had found a new respect for the ladies of the household. He certainly had.

Picking up the young woman, he held her while the staff cleaned the bed and then turned on the bath. He hadn't planned on joining her in the bath—she wasn't his mate, but she was beautiful. His plan was to put her in the tub, clothing and all, and then let someone else take over. But Opal saw him headed that way and nearly took his head off with her sword.

"What the fuck is wrong with you?" He let a little of his own beast take him while he yelled at the woman. "You could have hurt me badly, you moron."

"You are not taking my sister."

All kinds of things ran through his mind, none of them very nice. But he wasn't feeling it right now and slashed out with her with his dragon's magic.

He knew that she'd not die, but he did encase her in diamonds anyway. It was all he could do not to slam his tail against her and break her to pieces. Instead he entered the bathroom, put the woman in the tub, just as he'd planned, and left the room. Then he left the house.

There wasn't anything he wanted to do more than to fly. But he'd been warned that there might be poachers around, so he only took off running for the woods. Dana had been running for pleasure—in meets, yes, not just for fun—for a long time. And he found that while not as relaxing as sailing through the skies, he did love the feeling of getting his heart pounding.

You all right? He told Hanson that he was. *They're a little protective, don't you think? I mean, that Opal, she could beat a bear with a switch, I think, and come out on top.*

I think you might be right on that. They both laughed, and Dana slowed his steps. *I wonder which one is my mate. I know that one of them is. I just don't know if I want any of them, to be honest.*

I heard you telling Kip that one of them was. Speaking of which, he's as odd as ever, isn't he? Dana laughed and stopped by a felled tree. Sitting on it, he looked around for inspiration. *Are you still dabbling in stones? You know, making things from granite? I'm in need of a slab of it for the kitchen. Quinn wants to make candy, and I guess that is the best material that you can get.*

I have some at the house that are being brought here. Do you care what color? I have a pink one and one that has about ten different shades of gray it in. And no white at all. Very rare. Tell her for a box of candy, I'll give it to her.

Hanson laughed. *You should know that she's going to open herself a nice restaurant soon. Not just with candy, though all of it is really good, but also sandwiches and fruits. I think it'll be a nice addition. Her sister is going to help her with it too.*

I'll be her first customer. I've never had chicken fried steak before, but I think there wasn't any better than hers. As for the slab, as soon as it arrives, I'll make arrangements to have her come see it. But for now, I'm working in jewelry again. I missed it. He pulled out his phone and took some pictures of some of the things in the woods. *You know, I have an idea that I'd like to open a branch here. You think there is any kind of need for a very expensive jewelry shop?*

He didn't have any need for money. With as old as he was, and the fact that he could have diamonds any time he needed them, he was very wealthy. Not as rich as Danburn or Hanson, but he'd never have to work again if he didn't want to.

17

I think you should do it. Setting down roots here. Also, you have to look at this house that is perfect for you. It's a Tudor. And the back end of it has been added onto a few times, so it's massive. Also, and you're going to love this, it has a couple of turrets. Not just a little one either, but worked into the design, and the bottom part of it looks like it could be the dining room area. Hanson laughed as he continued describing the house. *I think the sucker has like nine bedrooms or more, plus this dining room that will open up to hold about two hundred mingling guests. Like I said, it's big.*

When can you get me in to see it? They were still laughing when he said that he'd take him today. *All right. Also, the stuff I have in storage — I don't suppose there is a place I can have it stored here until I can purchase said home, is there? It's not going to be any trouble storing it. It's just that my lease is about up at this place, and I didn't want to have to pay a full year for something I don't need.*

He did have money, but he was also smart about what he had, never overspending on things he didn't need. When he could, he'd fly for himself rather than to take a plane. He also bought pieces that he wanted on sale, at tag sales and auctions. Dana was very frugal. Not cheap, but prudent.

The house is empty and has been for about a year, I was told. The brick is brown, the roof of it is all slate, which is a big seller for me. And plenty of wooded grounds. There is also a stable with several paddocks and a big barn. He asked Hanson why he didn't buy it. *I don't need it, my dear fellow. I have a wife and a home that I love dearly. Mostly the wife. And a child on the way. I did think about buying it, but I didn't want to spend the money on it. I'm like that, you know.*

You are not going to tell me that you're broke. He said that he wasn't, but he loved that his wife was making them more money. *Jackass. All right. I'll meet you back at your house in about an hour. I want to check on Em, and then I need to get a shower. I needed some time out in the fresh air.*

I wish we could be more secure around here about the dragons. It would be nice to just go fly instead of waiting on the weather. He agreed with him. *All right, one hour at my house. See you soon.*

Instead of going in the house, he made his way to the car. If there was a problem, someone would call to him. Right now, even the thought of meeting his mate was too much for him. So instead of telling anyone where he was headed, he made his way to Danburn's house to get cleaned up. He wanted a place of his own, and the sooner the better. Not that Danburn and his lovely wife weren't the best sort of hosts and such, but he wanted his own things around him. It was time, he thought, that he really did settle down. Make roots, as Hanson had said to him.

Chapter 2

Sapphire knew the man was her mate. She wasn't thrilled about it, but he didn't seem to be either. He was a bully. Walking through the woods that she'd been enjoying for the last couple of hours, she revised her thought. Not a bully, but someone that stood up for himself. She thought of Opal and her snapping at him like a napless two-year-old.

Smiling, she thought of the man when Ruby had taken him to task as well. None of them had been very nice to him. Even when she'd realized who he was to her, she'd not defended him, nor had she thought to tell anyone who he was. She knew from Em that Dana could smell his mate on her skin, which made it odd, she supposed, knowing that one of them could be his. And then it turned out to be her. The youngest of the four.

As she wandered along the lake that seemed to be a part of the castle walls, she wondered at the strength of a dragon to make such a place. Not only that, but to have the land and the stone do what he wanted, even today. Like the walls with

21

light switches and hanging lights. She wondered if there were wires to such things, or just the illusion of them. Sapphire knew the story as well as any dragon did.

Danburn had wanted a home for shelter and to keep his family safe. The earth said that she'd gladly help him, but he told her that it must be a fair trade. And Sapphire thought that the land surrounding the area of the castle had done as well as, if not better than, Danburn had. The place was stunning.

The trees were healthy and full of life. There was an orchard in the back of the land, a place she'd only just left, that was full of blooms, the trees just starting to ready themselves for summer. The cherries were just beginning to ripen, and she knew that in a few days the staff and the town would be out there picking them. Jams would start to show up. Pies too. She knew too that the cook at the large castle would be making pie after pie to freeze so that they'd be eaten year-round. Something that she would bet had been happening for centuries.

The large Tudor house came into view several minutes before she was out of the woods. The roof and turrets alone made her think of the dragon behind her, Danburn, and the one that she was mated to. Oh, to own such a place, to live as she had so many decades ago.

Standing at the edge of the tree line, Sapphire knew that she was off the properties that the others owned, but she couldn't help herself. She needed time away from the house and all the people there. And the house in front of her seemed to call to her.

There were several cars out front, but she knew that the house had been empty of occupants that lived there for some time. The aura of love and happiness that had once been there around it was nearly faded. She knew that wasn't always a sign that people dwelled someplace, but in this case, she knew that she was right. The house had been dying of cheerlessness for some time.

It startled her when Dana got out of the first car in the drive. He stood there, staring at her for some time before he put out his hand for her. She wasn't sure what he might know until he laughed.

"We might have better timing than most, I think. I was thinking of purchasing a house, and now that you're here, you might well like to join me in the search. Come now, let's have a look, shall we?" Sapphire didn't move, not afraid, but hoping he was as wrong as she was. "You're my mate, Sapphire. Come on and let's have a look at the house to see if it can suit you. I hope it does, but you'll have the final say in it."

"You think it will not suit you, but you will buy it only because it does me?" He shook his head, her temper taking her mouth over. "I won't be treated as a simpleton."

"I wasn't doing any such thing. Damn it. Are all you sisters like this all the time?" She felt embarrassment heat her face. "I don't know anything about you, but I will say that even from here, I love the house. However, I'm not a man that cares so long as there is a roof over my head, a soft bed, and a place for me to work. So far, this place has it all. What is it you desire from a home?"

"The same, but pretty. I have lived so long in only caves that a home sounds good. I have not.... I'm sorry I was rude before. I think it has a lot to do with living with three other women and no one else. Especially as they're my sisters." He didn't point out to her that they'd all been rude to him but

23

thanked her. She might not have been so kind had it been her being the victim in all this. "I'd love to see the house with you. But know this—I'm very vocal about my likes and dislikes, and will tell you if I like it or not and why."

"I'd not have guessed that had you not told me." He was teasing her, something that most men never did. "Hanson was going to come here with me, but he got detained at home. I'm not sure by what, but he said he'd come over later if he was able. With this man, I've forgotten his name, you would do well to tell the man that we're married, I think. He has it in his head that I'm a young bachelor in need of a wife. Mostly his daughter."

The man came out of the house and looked at her. The disappointment on his face made her nearly laugh. She wondered if the daughter looked like her father, because that could explain why he wanted her to marry anyone that he worked with. Or anyone else, for that matter.

"You did tell me that you had someone in your life, didn't you, Lord Blankenship?" He said that he had. "You and the missus, you ready to see this place? It's the best we have on the market right now. Twelve bedrooms, dining hall, as well as a large dance room. The dance room can be converted into a...."

Sapphire tuned the man out in favor of looking around the house. It was a beautiful home. The front entrance alone had her wanting to live there, with its parquet floor and beautiful hand painted mural of what she could only guess was the forest beyond the house in fall. Touching her finger to the woodwork that surrounded the room, she knew that she could easily live there.

If he could see your face right now, I'd never be able to get a deal

24

on this place. You look like a woman that is in love. She grinned at him and moved to the library instead of the dining room where they were headed. *Are you going to wander around, or are you going to join us? We're supposed to be looking at this house together.*

The house calls to me. If you don't mind, I want to see what I can find out for you to talk him down. He asked her what part talked to her. *Everything. My goodness, you should see the view from the library. And there's a pool.*

Is it filled yet? I love a good swim in the morning. It loosens my inner dragon, so to speak. She told him that she could easily fill the pool for him should he want. *Yes. I'm just waiting for him to stop talking so I can make him an offer.* He laughed with her. *Or should we see the rest of the house before I sound too eager?*

The rest of the house. I've yet to find anything to make him think we're disappointed. And you're right, I have not a poker face when it comes to something I love. And I do love this house, Dana. She made her way to the next room, which just happened to be a gaming room. Sapphire told Dana about it.

A gaming room? Is there is a pool table, or just a room that you can play in?

She wandered around the massive room and told him about the bar too. *The pool table is here, as well as cues and plenty of other things that I can only imagine that goes with it. I've heard that they can be difficult to move, not to mention heavy. You think it was meant to go with the people and they have yet to return?* Dana told her what was on the paperwork. *Ah, so it's ours. Good. I'd love to learn to play pool. I've heard it's a very fun pastime for some.*

I have no doubt that you'd be very good at it too. He laughed again. *We're headed to the kitchen. Why don't you meet us there, if you'd like? Do you cook, Sapphire? I do, but not much. It's hard to make a meal for one, if you want to know.*

I do. And yes, I love to cook. Do you think there is time to put in an herb garden? He told her that there was one, and if it wasn't up to par, they could put in a better one. *Good, yes, I'll meet you in the kitchen then.*

She entered the room just as the men did from the dining room. The kitchen was modern and very up to date on the appliances as well. When she touched her fingers over the six-burner stove and double oven, all she could think about was how much fun she was going to have in there. Telling them that she had a nice butchers block that would fit in the room, if they were to buy it, she opened up the cabinets to find mouse droppings. Finally, something to tell him about that wasn't perfect about the house.

"Look, darling. There are mice." She faked a shiver and moved out of the way while the men looked. Reaching to Dana mentally, she mentioned how the mice would leave once they found a dragon in the house. "I don't care for little things creeping around."

"Oh, that is bad. My goodness. The cost of having an exterminator come in is going to be costly for a house this large." They played it up just enough, she thought. Then they moved into the pantry. "This is a place to store enough supplies that a person could have a grand party should they want to. It has places for extra plates and those carafe things that hold warm food."

She loved the shelves in the large room off the kitchen. There was a place for a washer and dryer too, she noticed. And when they wandered out of there, she opened the door to where she thought was the back yard, only to find a mud room, with a walk-in fridge and freezer. This kitchen was a dream, and she loved every aspect of it.

The upper floor was next. There were actually four levels to this house, not including the basement. But her heart was set on the room with the turret. Sapphire knew that a bed would look beautiful sitting in there. The realtor followed her into the room with Dana.

"The uppermost level is the master suite. There is also a small nursery. Not small, I would guess, but smaller than these rooms. It can be converted into an exercise room should you wish as well. There are more windows in the back of the house, as you can see. And all the bedrooms on this floor, as well as the one above it, have en-suite bathrooms, as well as large closets." She nodded, opening one of the large double closets and looking inside. She didn't care for the doors, said so, and made a mental note to get rid of all of the metal ones to bring in wood. The feeling of nature would be a large part of this house. "From here you can see the pool and the pool house. There is also a butler's cottage; as you can see, it is a smaller version of this home. And if you look to the left of the pool house, you'll see that there is play equipment. Not that I'm suggesting that you might have children; it was left when the previous owners vacated."

"There are a lot of left behinds, don't you think? Is there anything that we should know about this home? Like, did they up and leave it without taxes being paid? Are we going to have to pay more for the house to take the liens off? What is the problem that has such a large home sitting here falling into disrepair for so long?" He told her that mouse droppings weren't disrepair. "Perhaps not. But from here I can see that the roof on the pool house needs to be replaced. I can only assume that this one might as well. That is a large expense.

Then there are the floors in the living room. It looks as if the carpet has been stained recently, and there is a smell that makes me think of mold. I don't know that there is, but I have a good nose for things such as that."

The realtor looked at Dana, who told him to answer her questions. The house, as he could see, would be her domain if they were to purchase it. When the realtor started to sputter, she looked at Dana.

"I don't think we're going to get a good price on the house, darling. Perhaps we should go and find something from someone else. Too bad—I could see us here." The realtor stood there for all of a minute as they made their way to the front. He called out to them and Dana winked at her as they turned.

"I need to get this house off our books. The taxes are killing my small firm." Dana asked him how much the people were asking. "There is no family that is around. They were killed in an airplane accident several years ago. So yes, you can see that the house has been sitting here empty for some time, thus the repairs that need to be made on it and the mice. I'll make you a great deal on it."

He named his price and Dana asked if they could have a few moments. Then he lowered the house price by a substantial amount again. Then he told them his rock bottom price.

"That was much less than I ever thought I'd pay for any house, much less one of this size." She looked around the living room, the room they'd made it to when left alone. "What do you think? And there is no smell. What a thing to say to that poor man."

"Well, there is work that needs to be done. The doors to all the closets are metal. I would wish for wood, if you don't mind. Also, I'd like bigger windows, or perhaps a door to the decking from the dining room. It'll make the room much softer if we entertain. The pool house does need a new roof. But as you might have noticed, the one on the house is in very good repair. I flew over this house just last night." He laughed, then nodded. "Then there is the added bonus of the bedrooms being on separate floors, and a finished basement to use."

"Would your sisters live here?" The question startled her. "I know that you need to stay together to work. And if they should like to, then I have no problem with it at all. The only thing I should ask for would be a place I can call my own where I have no trouble or fights in there. My work requires concentration, and fighting and bickering would mess with that."

"You'd allow them to live here? With us?" Dana told her there was plenty of room. "I don't know what to say. I'll have to ask them, but I think they'd like that as well. You'll take the basement, yes? There is an outside entrance so they never have to go down there. In fact, you could close off the entrance from the kitchen and keep that area all to yourself."

"I'd like that."

He was being so nice. However, Sapphire thought that it wasn't him being nice right now, but he was like this all the time. A nice dragon. But she also figured that there was a beast, other than his dragon, just lurking below the surface, which would tear a person to ribbons should he cross him. And that it would take a great deal to make him lose his temper. But he'd be quick in his retaliation; that would be the only reason that he'd be brought forth in anger, she thought. Then he would be his normal calm self. To protect and to save.

His dragon would be a monster if she were hurt by someone, she thought.

~~~

As soon as the bank approved the funds being transferred to the holding company for the house, he called in some workers. There was no point in waiting, he thought. Dana started to tell them what he wanted, what he and Sapphire wanted, but figured that this part of the house should be left for her. Besides, he had his own things that he needed to get taken care of, like his offices in the lower level. He went there to see what he would need in the way of work. Dana was excited about this new venture of his.

Dana worked with natural light when he was working. He had always figured that since his jewelry would be in the outdoor setting more than not, he wanted it shown in the best way possible. And for his larger pieces, he would also use the light from outdoors with the indoors in mind as well.

The first thing that he wanted done was the two walls that were visible from the outside ripped out and replaced with floor to ceiling windows. Then he'd need to have a safe put in. One larger than the one he had at his old home. He would also need to have a security system put inside and out to keep them safe in the event someone figured out that he had gems around all the time.

Within hours, the house was being renovated and there were crews all over the pool house fixing the roof there as well. He knew that with money he could get anything he wanted done, and for the first time in a very long time, he spared no expense to have things just the way Sapphire wanted them. Happiness, that's what he wanted from her, and damn anyone who teased him about being a pussy whipped mate.

Laughing, he went to find Sapphire.

"We need a staff. And for a house this big, we're going to need a lot of staff." She told him that she agreed, and he wasn't surprised that she wanted to hire some of the woodland creatures. As element dragons, they had a very firm relationship with all creatures, but the faeries were the closest of all of them. "All right. I don't care so long as one of them can cook. While I know that we both enjoy it, we do have other work too. Okay with you?"

"Yes. And since my sisters are going to be here, if they agree, then they'll supply the cook for us. They'll also chip in some magic for the food we eat. I know you eat meat, as do I, but we also need a great deal of green vegetables."

That was fine by him and he told her so. "So, now that we've spent an enjoyable few hours together, how about if we find a place for us to have some dinner, then go shopping? I don't have any furniture that would suit a house of this size. Mostly I've been hanging out at someone's house until they kick me out because I'm such a bore to be around. I do have things in storage, but those things are suited more for looking at rather than using. Older pieces that I've kept for one reason or another."

"I have a great many pieces that we can use and look at as well. Old as some of them are, we might be able to sell them off for something that is going on in town, a charity or something. Like you, I have a few things in storage too. Some things to help me with my job." She looked embarrassed for a moment. "What room do you wish for me to take?"

He thought about sleeping with this woman. Making love to her. But he also knew that she was tender in that department too. As in, she might have had sex, but it had been a very long time. There was no smell of male on her, and what little there was, it had faded to near nothing. This question, he also knew, had cost her a great deal to ask.

"I'll sleep in the lower levels, until we get to know each other. You take the master bedroom. I should like some input into how it looks, but so long as the bed is large enough for the two of us, and I have a place to hang my clothing, I don't care. Oh, and no pink." He laughed with her—it was genuine, as well as relief for them both. "I should like to have dinner with you this evening. And your sisters, if you'd like to invite them."

"I would, but I would really like to have a meal with you. As you said, we should get to know one another." Taking her hand into his, Dana led her out to the car. "Where would you like to go?"

"I have a place in mind that I think you'll love. I've eaten there a couple of times with Elissa, and enjoyed it very much." She asked if it was the Dirty Harry Diner. "Yes, I take it she's taken you there as well."

"She has. My favorite is the fried pickles. Who knew that something like that could be battered and fried?" They were both laughing as they made their way to the little diner. "I have a sudden craving for onion rings and a thick juicy burger for some reason."

To call it a restaurant would have been grossly overstating their business. It had about ten tables, several more out of doors, as well as a bar. The bar wasn't for drinks as one would think, but simply for more room to feed people. He loved the pictures on the walls too.

The pictures reflected the times. They started when the town was nothing more than a wide spot in the road. A few log cabins that served as a holding point for mail. There was a trader too, who dealt in not just deer and other pelts, but also beaver, as they were that close to the river.

There were others too, but the standing place that was forever in all the photos taken was some part of the castle. Either the turrets that were tall with flags or the family living there, always too far away or too blurry to be recognized. He was sure that was done on purpose so the town wouldn't know that they'd been the original owners all along. Now, however, he doubted that anyone cared how long they'd been there—Danburn was that good to the town's residents. Also, there were people standing in front of the large lake fishing for food for the family, he'd bet, or for the castle inhabitants themselves. All in all, there were no pictures of any of the kings and queens of the castle that could be made out.

Dana ordered a hamburger, something he had gotten very fond of over the decades, and Sapphire did the same. She ordered onion rings to his baked potato, and when the waiter walked away, they began to talk and share side dishes.

"I have had a lot of jobs over the years. I enjoyed making jewelry the most. But I've only recently started making larger pieces that I've had a great deal of luck selling off. It's something I do for relaxation, and since I have no deadline to meet, it fulfills something deep inside of me when it's done." She said that she'd seen some of his pieces. "Really? That's wonderful. I have all the gems—most of them I've bought, some were given to me, and then there are others, when I was first starting out, that I sadly admit to stealing. You and your sisters, you've been working less and less over the years, I've noticed."

"Yes, they are manufacturing the gems now, but it's

harder to manufacture what I make for some reason. And the opal has been manmade too, but it's not nearly as pretty, and I think people can see that. There are cheapened versions of all of us, including you." Dana nodded. "There is little that we can do about it, but when one of your pieces comes out, someone out there tries to make it cheaper and not necessarily better. Not to me."

"No, me either."

They talked mostly about what they wanted in the house. Nothing too personal was brought up, and he thought that he might like that better. It came to him that he wanted her, wanted to hold her, more than her hand, but he also needed to take things slowly. Not just for her, but for him as well.

This was going to be his only love for the rest of his life. And he liked her. Loving her was part of him, but he also wanted to have fun with her. Do things together that they both enjoyed. Like fishing. She said she loved the sport, and he did as well. There was nothing rushing him, so for now at least, this was fine with him.

Dana had his car there, but they decided to walk back to the house. Since he'd already paid for it and work was being done, they walked through it again, this time with the plan to make any more changes before they moved in. Or perhaps they could live there while things were being done; it was not like they didn't have everything they needed even while it was being renovated. He saw the contractor coming toward them and had to smile.

"Hey, Dana. How's it...? I'm sorry, miss. I didn't see you there. You must be the mate." Dana introduced Sapphire to Charlie Brown, the contractor on their project. She giggled and asked him if that was really his name. "Yes. My parents thought I'd have so much fun with it. It's not Charles, but Charlie. And I didn't, let me tell you. I was, and still am to this day, made fun of. And I even went and married a woman by the name of Lucy. Lucy Brown. My goodness, you should hear it all now. Thankfully when we had sons, we didn't go near the cartoon strip. My oldest is Sam and the other is William."

Dana had always liked the other man. He was in his mid-forties with a head of snowy white hair, and had the sense of humor of a man that had been made the butt of jokes his whole life and learned to live with it. Charlie was as good natured as his namesake, and just as goofy.

"I don't suppose you have a dog named Snoopy, do you?" He said that he didn't but laughed with her. "You're a good man. Thank you so much for making me laugh and doing this work."

Charlie wandered off with Sapphire to look at the kind of doors that she wanted in the house. Dana had hated the metal ones too. As far as he was concerned, when building a house, nothing should be metal when wood looked so much better. His phone was ringing when he made his way out on the master deck.

"I need some advice." He told Kip to stop wearing tennis shoes to every event that he went to. "Very funny. I was thinking that I need to make some changes in what I do. You know, stop being the playboy with a lady of the month on my arm."

"And you needed my advice on what, then? Sounds to me like you have it all set up." He said that part he did, but he didn't know what to do about a job. "A job, huh? What is it you're good at, other than charming the panties off of some unsuspecting female that gets too close to you? Or spending

35

money on things that you don't need nor do you really want, but it was shiny or something."

"You're a funny guy today. Did you get laid or something?" He told him what he'd done today. He'd bought a house and met his mate. "No shit. You bought a house?"

"Yes, we did." They were both laughing when Sapphire joined him again. "I must go, my friend. Find me when you get home and I might have some ideas for you. I've been having a great day, so I might actually be able to help you."

"I will. And seriously, congrats on the new mate. I'm sure that you guys will be very happy together." He told him he thought that they would.

"What is it you do? I mean, I know that you design jewelry—I've actually seen some of your work over the years, as I said, but what about it makes you so famous?" Sapphire's face turned red when he acted as if she had wounded him. "You know what I mean. Fine rings and bracelets can't make all that much money. Not in this market."

"I not only design jewelry, I also sculpt. The other day while walking in the woods, I came across a fallen log. That doesn't sound very nice, but it had this growth of moss on it and I saw a brownie coming out of the hole near it. All I could think about after that was this log laying in an otherwise dead-in-the-winter forest with a family of brownies living in it. I'm working on the family now. I think that they'll be blended nicely into the landscape so that you'd have to work hard at seeing them. Or at least that's my plan."

"What will you use to make them?" He told her that he'd use silver and pewter that could bend easily for him. And then use other gems around it so that it would sparkle like it was in the morning, still with dew on it. She told him she loved that idea, and asked him if she could give him sapphires. "Would you? That would be wonderful. I'm going hunting in the mountain tomorrow. You can come with me and we'll have a nice picnic if you'd like. And we can fly if you wish. Danburn said that it's okay when higher up there; the villagers can't see us from down in the town."

"I would love that. I'll make something for us and you go foraging." She laughed. "When my sisters find out that you've made them an offer to come live with us, you might have more than you ever wanted in the way of opals, rubies, and emeralds."

He thought that would be cheating, but he wasn't going to say no. It might be nice not to have to search for and try to negotiate for the gems any more. But that didn't mean he was going to do it. Dana didn't want them there for a price, just for family.

Chapter 3

"You're serious? Dana bought the Wilkins mansion and is allowing us to live there with the two of you?" Sapphire nodded at her sister, Opal. "I wasn't very nice to him the other day. I think that I need to talk to him about that. So, you can imagine my surprise when he's still going to be nice to us."

"None of us were nice to him. And did you give a gift to the young child that helped me? No, you did not. I went to take her mine and there was nothing there from any of you." Em eyed her sisters, knowing that they were selfish at times but sweet women. "She saved my life, as you well know. The iron was headed to my brain, and we know what would have happened to me should Carmine not have caught it."

"I meant to. I even have it here." Rolling her hands, bringing the magic forward with the gift, Opal showed them what she'd gotten for the child. Slivers of opal in every shade were covering a jewelry box for her. And her name, Carmine, was spelled out on the top in the dragon language. "I wanted her to have something that she could remember me by. And

39

now that we're staying, I can get to know her better. And I just love the other women as well. Elissa kind of scares me, but at least she's not trying to harm us. You know as well as I that it's been a long while since we've had such peace."

Em smiled as she showed them what she'd made for the child. "It's her birthday month too. I thought that having earrings and a bracelet would be perfect for her. And I've put a little extra magic on them to make sure that if they ever get lost, she only has to call to them by using her birthdate and they come back. No matter where it is." That was nice, and Opal wanted to put the same magic on the box as well. Ruby held out her gift.

"It's a red bird. See?"

They did, and it was beautiful. The entire bird was ruby, and the flaws or whatever Ruby had put in it to make it appear like wings and eyes were a very nice added touch. As soon as Sapphire touched her finger to it, the bird came to life, for just long enough to sing.

"Carmine is forever singing. I think that she sings more than I do. Even when she's just sitting there watching television." Sapphire asked about the other things in the palm of her hand. "This is a rose that I thought she'd enjoy. Em gave me enough to make the stem, and then I made her this; it's a shard made of magic. It will be the strongest way for her to be found should someone take her."

"She has been bitten by the dragons, and the wolf." Em told her that it was stronger even than that. And the redbird would be a very big part of it. "So, she must carry it with her at all times?"

"Nay, I will give it to her and it will settle on her body. I have asked her sister and father about it, and they are welcoming of anything to keep her safe." Em smiled at her. "And what did you give her, Sapphire? Something of yourself?"

"I have a piece of my scale for her." They were all shocked by the generosity of the gift. It was the greatest gift that one could give a person. "I have encased it in glass so that should she ever want to use it when she's older, she need only to break it and bestow a kiss upon it to have a child. It will work for her for the rest of her life."

They decided to go and see the little girl now. It was after school and each of them were excited to give her the gift. But almost as soon as they were invited into the big house, Sapphire knew there was trouble. Or something that a child would think of as trouble.

"They're having a mother/daughter thing at school." Sapphire asked if Quinn wasn't able to go, thinking that she'd gladly take her place. "She's not my mother, and the rest of the kids made fun of me."

"Did you hurt them?" All of them turned to Em. "Well, it's a good question. I'm not saying that she should, but I might have. Stick them right in the —"

"Emerald. She's not going to do that." A low growl made Em smile when she told them that she was only trying to help. "See that you help her less about her human problems. We don't want the bad guys to know if word got out."

"He's still coming, you know." Sapphire asked if she knew who he was. "No. Somebody from a government office. My mom called them before we came here. She was trying to figure out what made me like I am. They were going to do all kinds of tests on me, but Mom got worse and we came here when my sister was hurt. We've come up with that I use almost all my brain."

41

"Okay, so someone is coming. If you can help us with who he might be, we can delay him. Not stop him—we can't mess too much with the fates—but we can sort of muddle with when he is to arrive." Carmine described him as best she could. "We'll all keep our eyes out for this man. And if you need us, you know to call with your gifts."

They had given her the gifts when they found out about the tea that was coming up. But when Sapphire reached out to Quinn about it, she somehow got Elissa instead.

Mothers tea? Oh my, they're still doing that? I would love to go. She told her about the issues she was having at school. *I wouldn't have expected that from the pack school. But then children will be children. Not that it makes it any less painful to her, but it's going to be easy to fix, I think. I'll talk to Quinn. Perhaps she and I both can go. I'm officially her grandmother, and I know that Quinn is planning for the adoption paperwork to be finished soon. Maybe by then, it'll be official.*

She's very upset about it. Elissa said that she would be as well. *I've tried talking to her, but she's more worried about the man coming. Did she tell you about him?*

Yes, in a vague sort of way. I think only one has her concerned. To me it should if he's doing this on his own. I hope so. I can't take much more of this. Why don't they just leave that little girl alone? Elissa was just as aggravated as the rest of them, she supposed.

Going to the garden that was being worked on at the back of the house, Sapphire and Carmine sat down on the bench while her sisters fought over who was going to plant something first. It was always a competition to them.

"My sister is going to have a baby. I don't know what it'll be to me." Sapphire asked her what she meant. "Will it be my half-sister or my stepsister?"

"Why does it have to be anything other than your sister?" Carmine looked at her. "Did you know that they're all my sisters? That we were born on the same day in the same year, each of us have a different creator."

"You mean father." Sapphire told her no, that they were dragons, some of the few first ones. "So, you're very old like Uncle Danburn?"

"Yes. His grandmother was one of the founding mothers to us all. Her and a group of women, all very smart and strong in their magic, created the rules and regulations that we all abide by. Well, we're supposed to abide by them. There are plenty of dragons that don't still. But Danburn, because of who his relatives were and that he is the strongest dragon ever born, he is the king." She looked out over the land, remembering it when it was nothing but a speck on the earth and in poor shape to boot. "We used to be friends with the humans. Helping them with whatever they needed. Then when it was apparent that dragons had tears of gems, the humans wanted them. And the dragons. So, someone decided that there had to be something, some one person, to make it so that the humans could find the gems that they cried without them killing the dragons. Or holding them captive." She looked over at her bickering sisters when Carmine did. "The first time that she was out in the world to plant the gems, put them where the humans could find them, it was difficult for the dragon to figure out what sort of gems to leave behind. And it was very draining on her to make sure that each kind could be produced. So back to the drawing board to work on that. The three of us were created and added to the first to make the gems that were sought after. It only took them one day to figure out what needed to be done. I have seen governments take years to make a single decision."

"Did it do any good? Having the four of you instead of just the one?" Sapphire pointed out that they were still there. "But you don't think it will be all that special to them anymore, do you? You're sort of losing your job."

"Yes. We are, sadly, and it's getting harder and harder for humans to realize the difference between real and fake. I can tell, as will you be able to when we show you, but a great many people can't. So, the cheaper versions of us, the emeralds, diamonds, and rubies, are becoming harder and harder for us to beat because of how cheaply they are made. Not to mention, they're perfect every time. Ours have flaws, but to me, that's what makes them beautiful. No one wants them any longer." She asked about the opal. "The opal hasn't been reproduced as well as the others have because they have certain colors to them. Like on your box. Those colors are ones that Opal made just for you. The way it spells out your name on the box, that took a great deal of her magic, and I would think that she had to rest for several hours after that."

"What language is this?" She told her it was dragon. "Is it hard to learn? I think I'd like to learn it someday. I've only heard it spoken once, and that was when I was in the living room when Uncle Danburn smashed his thumb putting the baby bed together."

"It's doubtful he knew you were there or he might have used one of the other languages that he knows. Dragon is only spoken to other dragons. And while you have a great many of them around here, they will not know to respond to you as such. You are not wholly human any longer, Carmine— you are an immortal. However, you are still a human to us."

Carmine said that she was useless. "Nay, you are never that. Without you, my sister would have died. And from what I have heard from the others, you have been a great deal of help rounding up others that would want to kill our kind. And you have something very special with what you can do. You require no magic. Iron will never bother you. You can use your powers with or without the help of the earth. Those things are important to our kind. Without magic, the earth wind and fire, there is no way that Danburn could have built his home, met and married his one true love. There is magic everywhere—you have a bit, but you are unique in that you were not given it but made it all on your own."

"Thank you for that. I was feeling sorry for myself, and my sister said that's not the way to get things done." She put her hand out when Sebastian joined them on the deck. "He's the most beautiful creature I've ever seen. And people think that he isn't real. But I have one right here in front of me."

The rest of the afternoon was spent with the young girl running around the yard with her pet. Sebastian, not usually fond of humans, seemed to enjoy the little girl, and was very gentle with her.

The sisters were still working on the garden. And while they were still arguing over what herbs to plant and where to plant them, her sisters had included Carmine when she came back to see how they were doing. It was a lot of fun watching her try and get her sisters to be reasonable, and more so when they finally quit in a huff and Carmine took over. She was ordering them around like a pro.

I've been thinking. She smiled when Dana spoke to her. *A date night shouldn't be over hot dogs and burgers. I think we should have a real date with real cloth napkins. That way when we get up, there is an air of celebration in the air, and the staff isn't wearing dirty black aprons. And when a tray is dropped, the hounds from hell aren't laughing and making fun of the waitress.*

That had happened the other night when they'd been out. The poor girl had not just dropped a tray, but it had been filled with an entire table of dirty dishes. Also, there were wine glasses as well as beer steins. It was much too heavy for her to carry in the first place.

What would we be celebrating? He mentioned several things, but the one that stuck in her heart and mind was meeting her. And him her. *I like that idea. Yes, we should do it. You'll have to let me know when to be ready, as well as what sort of dressing up we're doing. I can do formal wear all the way down to a pair of shorts and a dirty tee.*

How soon can you be ready? Sapphire said that she only needed seconds, because like him, she could think of her clothing and have it on. *Good. I'll be by to pick you up. Where are you anyway? I'm home and you're not here. I checked, even under the bed.*

I'm at Hanson's home now. We came over here to give gifts to Carmine for her help in saving Em's life. He laughed and said that was very sweet of them. *Yes, well, you might want to think of ways to close off your work area from them. My sisters have agreed to live with us. They're gathering things that they'd like to see in their rooms. And so you know, they don't need anyone to clean up after them. I forgot to mention that they all have their own magic and sometimes practice it in their rooms. Sebastian is Em's helper, I think the only one you've met. Mine is a cat. Not a cat, I guess, but a lemur; his name is Purr. You'll meet him tonight. He's been doing work for me. Wrinkle is with Ruby, and he's a three-headed jackal. Opal has an eagle, but he doesn't come into the house much. Not unless she needs him. His name is Rom.*

Great. Will I have one as well? Or do I use Purr? What a lovely name for a lemur, by the way. She told him how there was a list of them that wanted to work with him. *You know, that sounds like a blast. I'll pick one later with your help. So, let's go out to dinner. I have the entire date planned.*

Should I be afraid? He told her never, not with him. *I believe you. You're a kind man, aren't you, Dana? And a romantic. I've never met anyone like you before.*

I don't think I am, but you never know what others might think of as kindness. As for being a romantic, thank you. I think you bring that out in me. And I might just be a sap where you're concerned. She told him never. *I'll see you soon. I love you, Sapphire.*

With that, he closed the connection.

~~~

"My lord." He looked up from his desk to see an unfamiliar man standing there. Just behind him was another man, and two more behind him. They seemed to be of the same dress and facial expression. "We're here on behalf of a very wealthy man. He wishes for you to help him in contacting a woman by the name of Emerald Smith."

"Why do you think I'd know anyone by that name?" He called to Sapphire and told her who was here and what they wanted. Though he didn't really know either, but he was worried, as all of them were upstairs at the moment.

"We believe that she lives here. With you." Dana leaned back in his chair and regarded the man while trying to think. When nothing came to him, he called out to Danburn and the rest of the dragons. "She is worth a great deal of money to this man, and he wishes for your help to talk to her. There is no harm in a little conversation, now is there?"

47

"He wants me to let him talk to her? Sounds.... Well, I'm not sure how that sounds, but it certainly doesn't sound legal. Why doesn't he just call her up and talk to her? I can find her phone number out for you if I ever meet her. As I said, I don't have any idea what you're talking about." Danburn said he was with Rette and Hanson and they were on their way. Dana thanked them. "Why, again, do you think that she's here? I mean, you have to have a reason to come into my home, uninvited, and think that I'm going to cooperate with you in any way. Trespassing in a man's home is a serious offense."

"You have her here. I have seen her upon the grounds." Dana said nothing, but the men spread out in the room. There weren't four of them, as he'd thought, but as they continued to multiply, he began to think he was in more trouble than he had thought. "We wish for you to retrieve her for us and allow us to take her. We will not be thwarted again, Lord Blankenship."

"Thwarted? I don't know how you came up with that, but I do know that you're not being honest with me. As of right now you've lied to me twice." The front man shook his head, confusion all over his face. Actually, it was on all their faces. They were the same faces too. Right down to the little wart on the end of his nose. "You said that you *believed* she was here, when in fact you knew she was. Or so you said. Okay, then you said you wished to talk to her. Now you want to take her too. Taking a person against their will is a very serious crime in and of itself. That isn't just a lie, gentlemen, but also against human law."

The door opened and there was Danburn in all his glory. As soon as he bellowed *"Be gone,"* the men, all of them, were gone, save the one that had been talking to him. Danburn walked right up to the man, picked him up by his neck, and shook him hard.

"Melville, what are you doing on my family's lands? And you dare to send minions of yourself instead of coming here and talking like a person should? I should have you arrested and then put in irons. You moron. You scared us all with your tricks and sleight of hand. Show yourself now. Where are you?" He shook him harder this time, then threw him across the room. The man landed with a hard thud but didn't get up. "I asked you a question."

"I want the emerald dragon. I saw her first, and I want him to bring her to me so that I can have her as a pet. You have taken all the good ones, Dan—Lord Danburn, and I think that you have more than enough special ones on your side." The roar took his breath away. Dana nearly fell to his knees when Danburn drew in a deeper breath to do it a second time. "Please, I beg of you. Don't hurt me again."

But it wasn't a roar, it was a name, said in a language so old that he'd nearly forgotten that he could, at one time, speak it. The language of their kind.

The man that appeared in the room was dressed all in blue. It wasn't until he moved that Dana realized that it wasn't blue at all, but purple. Royal purple, and he felt the urge to bow before him even before he said his name.

"Lord Danburn, I'd like to—" Danburn corrected him. "Marquess English, Lord Danburn, I hadn't been informed of your title change. Who died?"

"None of your business. What right do you have to be here, Baron Melville James? And even more so, why are you sending in duplicates of yourself instead of coming to talk to me directly? Does this have anything to do with the council looking for you? I told them that I'd bring you in, but they said that they wanted to talk to you first. So you understand me, if you dare send yourself here like that again, to any of the houses that I consider to be family, I shall take you to task, and that will not bode well for you." Baron James waved him off, as if Danburn wasn't just higher on the food chain than him, but would gladly have him for dinner, quite literally. "What reason have you to come here, looking for a pet, as you called her? The emerald dragon is here, but she is no longer your concern. You're to stop looking for her. You have been warned, Melville. Unless you wish for me to—"

"Not my concern?" Baron James or Melville, or whatever his name was, looked at Dana, then back at Danburn. "She will forever be my concern. I'm the one that wounded her. Not wounded her, but was playing around when I accidently hit her with a shard of iron. No harm meant, but I would like for you to bring her to me now."

"You wounded one of my dragons?" He said that she wasn't his and it was an accident. "Why were you playing with iron? I made it perfectly clear the last time I spoke to you that you're not to dabble in things such as that. And when I tell you that she is no concern of yours, that is what I mean. Stay away from what I consider to be my family, Melville, or you'll be hurt. She is family, and family does not get harmed nor kidnapped while they're a part of what I consider mine."

Sapphire came into the room then, and even Dana could tell that Baron knew who she was. As Baron reached out to touch her, Sapphire put out her hand and his arm from wrist to shoulder turned to stone. A blue sapphire stone.

"You will not touch what I do not give you permission to touch, sir."

50

He took his arm to his chest and smiled. Dana could almost see him thinking. A blue sapphire dragon as well as an emerald? In the same house? And his proof was right there in his hand. His sapphire hand. But little did he know that as soon as he left the property, his hand would be normal other than a slight blue tint that looked as if he was dyeing himself.

"You are very beautiful, my dear." Dana stood up and let a little of his dragon go, but not enough so that he'd know that there were five such dragons in the house. He wasn't even sure that Danburn knew that the others were here and what they were. "What could I pay you, Danburn, for such a prize? Come now, you have your price. Everyone does."

"She's my mate." That had all of them turning to him. He was sure that it was his tone; he let his beast talk for him. "Touch her again, or even attempt to touch any of my new family, and I will kill you. No threat, Melville, but a promise you might well take to the grave with you. This is my mate. And the sister you want, she's not to be touched either. They're under my protection from now on, and I will kill you should you harm any of them again. Do you understand me?"

"Your mate is yet untouched by you, Lord Blankenship. So, as far as I can see, she is free for anyone to take." His laughter did nothing to calm his dragon. "I think that I shall petition to Lord—no, sorry, Marquess English—and see about just simply taking her as she is. And you cannot force her to mate with you, now that—"

Danburn disappeared. Just within a single blink of an eye, he was gone. Melville laughed, his laughter making it harder and harder for Dana to hold onto his beast for much longer. And when Melville went to Sapphire again, this time not touching her but making it look as if he wanted to, he smiled at her.

"I shall return, my dear. And when I do, we'll have such fun."

When he too disappeared, she looked at Dana.

"Come here." She shook her head. "Please. My dragon is getting more and more difficult to hold onto, and he needs to know that you're all right. Let me touch you, and that should calm him down a great deal."

"Where did Danburn go?" Dana told her that Danburn had gone away to give them time. "Time for us to be mated, you mean. So that Melville couldn't take me." He told her that was right.

When he held her in his arms, all he could think about was that his hands were being tied. And he was being forced into something that he didn't want. No, that wasn't right. He did want Sapphire, but not like this, not to force her into something that she'd never want.

"What do we do now? Have sex?"

The throat being cleared had him remembering that Rette and Hanson were still there. Looking at the two men, their faces red with embarrassment—or anger, he wasn't sure—he asked them what they were to do now.

"She had a good idea. But other than that, I'm going to have someone come and stay here, and then follow our buddy Melville." Rette looked at Sapphire as he continued. "I'm sorry, my dear. I know that this is going to be tough on you both, but we have to take precautions on this. He appears to be stupid, and stupid men make the worse kind of mistakes when they're angry."

"I know. I just thought, like Dana said, we'd have more time to get to know each other. I mean, we've only just met."

Hanson asked if what he'd said was true about claiming her. "Yes, he can claim me, but he has to have the permission of the lord of the realm that I'm living in. It has to be formal, written out, and approved. Then he can take me or any of us at a moment's notice."

"So that leaves the others to be caught too." Dana told Hanson that he didn't think that he knew of all four of them, just Sapphire and Emerald. "You have them all here? Christ, man. And in college you could never get a date."

"Funny. But I do have an idea. I'm not sure how the others are going to like it, but it might buy us some time." Ruby and Opal entered the room, and he had a feeling that even this plan wasn't going to work. When they were all five together, they shone, like a bright beacon that would draw anyone there. "I need protection around the house so that no one may enter without permission from Danburn. Also, I would like for you both to touch all of them so that in the event he tries to take one of them, we can find them. Because of the kind of dragons that we are, just a touch is all that it'll take."

"Done." He looked at the woman who had entered the room. "I am Lady Beatrice. Lord Danburn sent me to help you. I am the lady witch that has helped him as much as he has me. What else do you need, my lord?"

It took them several hours to get things managed. He was right, neither of the other sisters liked his plan. But when he pointed out that they had to think of something better, they decided that this was the only way. To avoid giving themselves over to James, they agreed to hide where Dana said. In plain view of them all.

Now he needed to talk to Quinn and see what she knew. The woman was a walking encyclopedia of dragon lore and information. She would know the loopholes. Because he knew as well as they all did that there were loopholes to every set of rules ever made. Usually to help out the one writing them. Danburn contacted him just after they were settling down to dinner.

I will not be returning until this is settled and you've taken a mate. Em will be safe if he asks for them both because he'll have to petition all over for one of them. I could keep him busy for months. For now, I have gone to my home in.... Perhaps it would be best if I didn't say except that for now, he'll not find me. What is your plan? He told him what he was thinking of doing, what he'd done to the women other than Sapphire. *Brilliant. I'm going to assume that Beatrice has shown up? My mother will be there soon too. She has something to add to your plan.*

I didn't want this to be done this way, Danburn. We're getting to know each other, having fun with what we want to get ready for the house. He told him he was sorry. *If you could explain to me about the men, I'd be very happy about one thing. What the fuck were they?*

Minions. A small part of Melville that can be duplicated over and over. When confronted with information or even a little question that they weren't given the answer to, as you noticed, they get confused. They are of one body and mind but can block a person into a corner so that they cannot get out. Thusly killing them. Why he thought it would work on you, I have no idea. Melville isn't a dragon, but one that plays in the dark arts. A man that can do one bit of magic and nothing more. He's shown his hand in this. He can't do a lot of tricks, for which I'm grateful. All he can do is make many of himself, but that is dangerous enough. Dana asked him how old he was. That could be a reason to be fearful of him, if he was terribly old and powerful to go with it. *Not too much older than a hundred or so, I think. I never cared for the man, and I didn't check on him as I should have.*

So, he's nothing more than a blow hard that makes himself seem bigger than he really is. Danburn agreed with him. *If I remember correctly, a man such as him was one that would empty the barn of dung from the horses on an estate. Or chamber pots of the queen of the castle.* Danburn said that was right. *So, he's nothing more than a shit man.*

Pretty much. But he is no less dangerous for what he can do. Remember, he can duplicate himself. So, he could be in many places at once. Your home, mine — well, not mine, but he could be anywhere. Take care that he doesn't catch the women. If he does, then there is no telling what would happen to Lady Earth. Dana said he would be careful with all the women at his home. *See that you do. I don't want to lose anyone, and not my dear friends. Especially to a fool.*

Chapter 4

Sapphire wasn't sure what to do. Be sexy? There was no point in it, she thought. He'd have to take her, today if she was to be safe. Looking at the flowers on her vanity in the bathroom, she wondered if anyone in the world would know that they were her family.

Beatrice had turned each of them into a bauble. An everlasting one, she called them. Her sisters were now in an opal vase with a blue and red rose, seemingly made of glass. The green of their stems was of the finest emerald, their heads, the most picture-perfect roses, were of old dark ruby and a blue sapphire. A bit of her own body had been added to complement the disguise should it be seen in the room. They sat in a vase made of opal; her sister had never looked finer in all her glory.

Touching her fingers to them, she knew that they were as safe as they could make them. The magic that held them to the vanity prevented them from being broken or stolen. She loved Dana for thinking of something so clever and safe. And even though no one thought it would work, it had, and they were going to owe him such a gift when this was all said and done.

"Hello. Are you all right?" She turned and smiled at Dana, her robe suddenly feeling too big. "I'm sorry about this. I had meant to take our time, to get to know each other better. But you do know that this is the only way that we can do this, don't you?"

"I know. I had no idea that he could do that either. I mean, I guess I did know that we could be captured, but not that he had to—" Sapphire grinned at him. "I'm babbling again. I do that when I'm nervous."

"You're very lovely when you babble." She walked toward him and noticed that he was fully dressed. Asking him about it didn't help her nerves. "I'm going to seduce you first. Then make love to you as I've wanted to since I first met you. Just because we have to be rushed doesn't mean that we can't enjoy this, correct? I'm not a 'wham, bam, thank you, ma'am' sort of man, as you'll find out."

"I'm afraid. Not of you, but all this. I had no idea when Em was hurt that it would bring such troubles down on your head. I'm not regretting meeting you. I have fallen in love with you and everything about you." He told her it was all of them now, not just her and her sisters. "I don't want any of you hurt. I wish that we'd.... No, I'm glad that we met, as I said. Had we not, then none of us would have been safe, and Em would have surely died. I already owe so much to this family and you. I'm not sure I can ever begin to repay you."

"You don't have to, but I have an idea how you can make me very happy. And I wanted to tell you how very much I love you." He bent on one knee and pulled her hand to his mouth. When he kissed her, she watched as he pulled a small black velvet bag from his pocket. Whatever was inside, it was heavy, and she felt her belly clench up just a little.

"You don't have to do this, Dana." He told her that he most assuredly did need to do this. "I'm in love with you now—marrying you isn't necessary."

"Hush. I've been working on this for you. I had to use the supplies that I had on hand to keep you from knowing what I was about. But it's something that I wanted to give to you soon. I just had to hurry it up a little bit more." He opened the bag and all she could see of it was that it was a wide band. When he slipped the ring on her finger, her breath caught. "I love you, Sapphire. I have for a very long time, I think. Since I saw my first untouched sapphire, I knew that you'd have a heart of gold and a beautiful outlook on life that I would love to be around. You are my heart, Sapphire. My love, my everything. And if you would consent to marry me, I've permission from the king, because of what you are, to marry you post haste. Will you, will you marry me, my queen?"

"Yes." She laughed when he kissed the ring then let her see it. "Oh Dana, it's beautiful. I've never seen anything so beautiful in all my life."

The band was wide, but he had made it that way to hold the gems that were on it. And the dragons. There were two of them. One of them was a brilliant blue, like hers was when she had an occasion to shift. Her body was beautiful, his too. The two of them wrapped together to hold the diamond in the middle of them, their claws holding the gem.

When he stood up, he kissed her. She loved the way he took his time, the way he tasted to her. His hands moved over her body, touching parts of her that she did every day. But he made her feel special, like she was important and that she mattered. Not just to him, but to every living thing there was. Lifting his head from her, she knew that she would love this man forever, that he'd make her safe and secure, but most of all, he'd love her. Unlike anyone ever would.

"I love you, Sapphire. Everything about you." He kissed her again, before she had time to say anything back to him. "You are the heart and soul of my life. The reason that I get up in the morning, the reason that my heart beats. My breath comes in and out of my lungs."

She tried to think, to process what he was saying, but all that she could do was feel. Him, his hands, the words that seemed to spread over her body. And when he kissed her again, taking every bit of her air out of her lungs and replacing it with his own, all Sapphire could think about was that she loved him. That he loved her.

The bed touched her back. How she got there, she had no idea. Just knowing that he was going to join her, to make love to her, threw all other thoughts out of her mind. When the bed moved, he was there. Rolling into his embrace was like coming home to her.

"I love the way you respond to me. The way that your eyes darken with passion. Your lips seem to beg me to kiss them." She looked into his eyes, seeing his dragon there as she was sure that he could see hers. "She's right there. I can see her. She's as beautiful as you are."

"I see yours as well. And his love for me." Dana kissed her again, his mouth moving down her throat to her pounding pulse. When he nipped at the skin there, she knew that he'd drawn blood. The small and unfulfilling climax made her want more, need more. When he licked her throat, she moaned loudly so he could hear what he was doing to her. "You're driving me over the edge."

"Oh, honey, we've only come to the edge. I have so much more to drive you there and over. We'll go together." She knew he was naked now; his thick hard cock brushed against her belly and then her leg as he moved down her body. "I'm going to drink from you until I'm satisfied. Then I'm going to take us to such heights that your dragon will be jealous."

"She already is." There was no more air for conversation after that.

He ate her like a man starved. Like a meal that he was going to savor forever. Every time she came, he told her more, and his tongue entered her so deeply that she knew that part of it was his dragon. And when she begged him to stop, he seemed to double his efforts. Sapphire was sure that he was going to kill her, right then and there. And while she found that she didn't care, she did need to feel him inside of her.

When he moved up her body she was exhausted, sure that she couldn't come again. But every inch that he moved his mouth over her body, he brought her again and again. Kissing her this time, his mouth tasting her, his touch was slightly rough in its search for more of her, and she moaned. His cock was so thick that she was sure that he'd never be able to fit inside of her. Then he was there.

Her scream wasn't from pain but pleasure. The most incredible pleasure that she'd ever felt. And when he moved, his body giving and taking, she hung onto his shoulders and wrapped her legs around his, sure she was going to be tossed away when she came again.

His body was so like hers in so many ways, yet very different. The taste of his nipples sent her into a frenzy of need.

61

The feel of his muscles in her hands was like holding onto a supple tree branch, its strength there for her to take should she want it. His chest was hairless, his skin was flawless, and there wasn't an ounce of fat anywhere on his entire body.

"Look at me." She had no choice in the matter, opening her eyes that she'd not even realized that she'd closed. "My dragon needs to take his part of you. A part that will make us whole."

Dana's voice was rough, harsh even. The dragon was doing that—she knew that he was just on the surface of Dana. And when his body, his mouth too, shifted, she felt the tear of his teeth, much smaller than the full dragon, as he tore into her tender flesh over her heart.

The bite was painful but wonderfully erotic. When he cried out that he was coming, telling her not just with his mouth that he was but his body as well, she let herself go, tumbling over the edge that he promised her, and simply slipped away on a wonderment of pleasure and happiness.

~~~

Dana rolled to his back, taking Sapphire with him. He'd never had sex like that before. His dragon had never been the sort to take him over when they were with a woman. And when he spoke to him, his dragon speaking to him for the first time in all of his life, Dana wasn't surprised at all. He'd come to think of him as a different being than himself anyway.

You are a good man. Dana laughed a little, the words surprising when he knew that he was not. *You are. A man with principles and morals. It is a great honor to be your other half. Thank you for finding our mate, and then allowing me to bond with her as well. She too is a good person, a perfect match to one such as you.*

I didn't know that you could talk to me as if we were in the same room. I know that Danburn has always been able to speak to his dragon, but I guess I just figured that because he was king, he could do that. Dragon said that he could do many things now that he'd taken a mate. *I see. Our mate, she's something else, is she not? And we're paired too, gem to gem. I never thought to find one so beautiful and so loving. Hell, I never expected to find her at all.*

I knew that she was out there; there is one for us all. Sometimes they are taken from us, but we have a mate. Finding her is the problem. You are so busy — all people are, I think. Sapphire. What a beautiful name as well. And her sisters, they are...I wish to call them a hoot, but its more than that. I have heard them when they bicker. I think they do that to have fun. He laughed when his dragon did.

Dana hadn't many friends in his life. Very few that he could count on. Danburn and the other men here, they were all he had. But looking at Sapphire, he knew that he could change that for her. Become more of a people person, as she seemed to be. Loving the world and everything in it.

I think you might be right about the sisters. But I love them as well, you know. They're wonderfully colorful, and so honest that it makes a man not want to ask their opinion on things. Dana rolled to his side, laying his bride on the bed next to him. Then he covered her with the sheet that had been tangled around them. *She is perhaps the most beautiful creature in the world. Even in her sleep I have come to love the way she looks. I think I'm turning into a sap.*

Nay, my lord. Just a man who is in love for the first time in his life. But her dragon will be magnificent too. I cannot wait to see her. He couldn't either. *We shall soar the skies, the four of us. No one will ever be a more gorgeous pairing, because of her.*

You're a little in love with her, I take it. He laughed a little. *I never thought to take a bride. She is more than I could have hoped for. But after so long, I thought me to be alone in my golden years. I think that we all did. And it only took Danburn to call us here, to our second home, for us to realize our fates. I wonder if the others will have their mates as well. If they're on their way here. They cannot be as beautiful as our Sapphire.*

What are golden years? Dana explained it to him. *I don't think that you will ever need a card when you're old. For I think us old now. And there will never be enough discounts for someone as old as us. If you were to tell them of your age, I think most would have you put into a sanatorium.*

Dana laughed again, feeling wonderful. *There is a man coming for the sisters. And our mate. We must be ever diligent to keep them safe. None of them are as safe as we'd hope. But they will be on their best behavior, I think, when it comes to making sure that they're safe. Don't you think?* He said that he did, and thought that if anyone could keep them safe, it would be all the dragons here. *I agree with you on that, and know you will watch them as well as myself. It's when she's not with me that I worry about.*

I think that I should worry more for the man who would try and take her from you. He is only a human, correct? Dana told him that he thought him to be part dragon. *Nay, I don't think he is. Otherwise he could not have been changed by the sapphire that touched him. Had she touched a dragon as such, he would not have been harmed by it. He is no more a dragon than the little girl I've come to cherish as well. Carmine, I think her name would be.*

Danburn told me once that he had some power, but not enough to take on a dragon. But that was a long time ago — perhaps things have changed for the man. I wonder what he's about? I wouldn't think that Danburn would make such a mistake. Maybe there is more to his magic than we first thought. Frowning, he got up,

64

dressed in soft clothing, and went to the window to think. *I'm sure that he is nothing compared to us. Danburn has enough magic that most dragons would only dream of it. Perhaps that's what makes Melville so hard to pin down. The fact, too, that he came into my house as he did. Duplicating himself over and over to intimidate me.*

Mayhap it is because I am a dragon all the time that I could tell what he has not the magic that he thinks he does. I'm not sure why Danburn hasn't realized that as yet, but this man, Melville, he is only human. Partial human, because I can smell the black magic of him. If you could touch him, I could tell you more. He said that he would, the next time he was near him. But asked him how, if he'd not touched him, could he tell. *I smell no black magic on him. But Danburn has touched him, my lord, as his human self. If I were to touch him, I'd more than likely crush him, but I could tell where the magic came from. Perhaps the witch or warlock that helped him had given him power once, and that is what Danburn had felt, and never thought to check him again.*

Now that I think about it, he's never touched any of us. Other than Sapphire, and all she did was touch him with her magic. The dragon said that wouldn't have happened had he been dragon. *What would have happened had he been a dragon then?*

He would have been solid. Like the sister was when you were angered at her. But when you released her, she was dizzy for a time, correct? He said that he didn't know, he'd released her from a distance. *It is the way of all creatures that you encase. They are solid from head to toe, as was the sister. But with a human, you will only encase what you touch. A human would not be able to breathe if solidly encased. I think that is the reason that the magic of a dragon affects them thusly.*

He wanted to find a human right now and figure this

out. The only one that he knew of was the gardener. Running down the stairs, careful even then to be quiet and not to wake Sapphire, he found the man in the kitchen.

After explaining to him what he wanted to do, the man asked him several times if he'd be hurt. Dragon told Dana that he'd not be, but to give the man diamonds for his payment. When he put out his hand, it was trembling, so Dana was very careful to only touch his finger.

It worked just the way Dragon said it would. Only his finger was frozen in diamonds. Careful to peel off several of the smaller stones, he took the magic off and handed the man his payment. He stared at them for several moments before he shook his head.

"I'm sorry if I've hurt you." The man said that he'd not. That it had been his honor to help him. "Then you should take the diamonds."

"I am but a poor man, Lord Blankenship. Very poor. My children have moved away, 'tis only my lady wife and myself. But if I come home with a handful of diamonds she's going to have my head. Then yours. I shall only take the one, if it pleases you." Dana was touched by the man's honesty and his words. "My wife is a good woman, and will make good use of the money we can get for it. But she'll wonder, you see, and I cannot have her thinking I've robbed myself a jail sentence."

"Nay, I can see that." Dana reached for his wallet and pulled out all the cash there. "This is a bonus for you, Mr. Crocket. For making the garden out back a splendid place for my wife."

Denny Crocket smiled and took the cash, thumbed through it, and kept only seventy-five dollars. Then he did the most incredible thing—he handed him back all the rest. Dana asked him why he'd only take that much.

"My wife wishes for a new stove. So far she's only managed to pinch herself enough off of each check that I bring her to pay for about half. As I said, we are poor as mice in a church." Dana nodded, unsure what to do. Then Betty, their cook, cleared her throat.

"I was wondering if he should move to the property, sir?" He smiled at her, knowing that she had already refused the butler's cottage; she and her husband had preferred to live in their own home. "It would be nice, should there be a trouble in the middle of the night, to have a man so close by to you. And it'll be good to have the house lived in too. Don't you think?"

"Oh no, I cannot live there, sir. It'd not be right for a man such as myself to live on a fine estate like this." Dana asked Mr. Crocket why not. "Well, it's a lovely home. I've nothing to.... Sir, it's not right for a gardener to live like that."

"Then it's settled." Laughing, he looked at Sapphire when she spoke, entering the room like the queen he thought her to be. "You and your lovely wife will move into the cottage. And when there is a storm and Dana is away, I'll know that there is someone close by that can help me with the power should it go off."

"My lady, I—"

Sapphire cut him off. "You will, Mr. Crocket, simply because I wish it. You don't wish to disappoint me, do you? And I have a small job for the lady wife too, should she wish it. There are going to be many herbs, thanks to you, and when the drying room is finished, perhaps she'll be able to help me with that? Not to mention there will be times when she can come help Betty when she needs it." Betty nodded and smiled at him with a wink.

"Mildred, she might like that, I think. You'd be well to use her items, my lady. She can make oils, lotions, and liniments too. There's not much call for homemade anymore, I guess, but she enjoys making them for gifts. If you've a mind to try them, you won't regret it. I've been using them on my hands since we were first wed." Sapphire touched her hand to his and she looked surprised. "See? Very soft, and me working like I do."

"I tell you what—you have your wife come and talk to me, and perhaps she and I can come to some kind of agreement about things." He said that he would. "Good. You are a joy, Mr. Crocket, and you will be moving into the cottage."

Sapphire kissed Dana on the mouth and left the kitchen. Mr. Crocket looked at him and then at the closed door that Sapphire had just left through. Shaking his head, not saying a word but smiling largely, he left the kitchen too and went outside. Life was never going to be boring around here, he thought.

"She'll have him thinking it was his idea by the end of the day, I'm thinking. That lady of yours, she's slick." He agreed with Betty. "And to think I was thinking you two might not need me. You do, to keep the ones she hires, that she doesn't really need, working to earn their keep. Why, a woman like her, she has no more need for a gardener than I do. And I don't have myself a garden anymore."

Dana was still laughing as he went to work in his offices. They were coming along nicely, and he was excited to be creating again. And the log project was just what he needed, he thought, to keep his mind occupied and not thinking of the man who might come to harm them.

The sisters were safe, he knew that, but he did worry about them. They had been put into a deep sleep, one that wouldn't harm them at all, but he still worried. They were his sisters too, as far as he was concerned, but he figured that having them as beautiful art was much better than having them chained to something and made to produce gems for the rest of their lives.

His offices were nearly finished, he saw when he entered his domain. But he had things that he could set up and put away to get a start on things. His gems were in a large safe, much like the ones that they used for guns. But with his wife here and her sisters, he thought it might serve them all better if he got in a bigger one. It was being put in when he went to the section of the basement that was being set up for it.

"Mr. Blankenship, it's a good thing we had to take out those walls there. We wouldn't have been able to get this in otherwise. I think the last one I saw that was this big was at the First National Bank in town." They had torn out the wall behind where the safe was going to go, and were fitting it into the sub-walling. By putting it back into the wall, it was going to be flush with the rest of them. Otherwise, it was going to take up a lot of room. He gave them a little help, letting his dragon have some fun with installing it. "Wow, don't think we could have done it without you. Thank you, sir."

"It was my pleasure. I cannot wait for this to be done. But I have to say, this is moving on a good deal faster than I thought it would. Thank you for that." The man said that he didn't mind at all, and his men needed the money. "Well good, I might have some other projects to do as well. The barn needs to be reinforced before winter again. Things like that."

"We've not had much of an occasion to work these last years. No one is building, and most people are trying to do the repairs or upgrades themselves. Hard times around here." Dana told him things were looking up. "Yes, sir. We've a bid on a couple of the projects coming around the bend too. Looking forward to being busy all the time."

After that, he went to the side of the room where he was setting up his tables and lights. The boxes were stacked up the way he wanted them, all together by light, and the shelves were put together already. So, opening boxes, not bothering yet with hanging anything, he was thinking of his log piece when Sapphire joined him with a picnic basket.

"Hey." She grinned and asked him if he was hungry. "Shit, I forgot. We can go right now. I can do this anytime."

"No. It's a dreary wet day and I thought we could just eat here. Besides, all the men are having lunch upstairs. Betty made soup and homemade bread. That's what we're having with our lunch too." He started clearing off the big table he was going to use as a work area as she continued. "I noticed that the windows are up. And the door looked fantastic."

"To be honest with you, I've been thinking about anything but windows. How have you been? Getting things settled up with Mr. and Mrs. Crocket?" She said that they had very little to move. "I thought that might be the case. I've had the crew go over first thing when I got here to make sure that it had everything they'd need. The stove and the refrigerator have been replaced already—they were in terrible shape—and the grounds are getting a good once over. I figure that he'll not want to mess with his own when ours is so big."

"Speaking of which, I'm going to have him hire a crew to take care of the orchard in the back. There hasn't been anyone caring for it for some time, and it looks it. There are apple trees, as well as peach and pear. I don't know what else. I was so saddened by the shape of the first part of the place that I didn't want to go any further in." He said to have him hire whoever he wanted. "I thought you'd say that. Also, his house is a rental, the one in town, did you know that?"

"No. I mean, I just assumed that he owned it since he was getting himself a new stove." She said that he'd been paying for things like that since they moved in. "That's not right. If there is a problem, then the landlord should know about it."

"I agree with you. But it's Danburn. I don't think he knows that he owns a row of houses, along with the buildings that he owns. There are about seven of them there, and most of them, if not all, need some kind of upgrades." Dana asked her if she'd told him about them. "No. I was kind of hoping you'd ask him to sell them to us."

"Why? I don't care if we own them or not, but I think you have a reason." She nodded and grinned at him. "Am I not going to like this?"

"Oh, it's nothing like that. What I was going to say was, we could own them, and when my sisters are sick of living here, which will happen, they can each have their own place to chill out. No one lives in four of the seven homes. Now five of them are empty. The lone two hold outs are one, a druggie, I think, and the other is a woman with five kids that should be living in something much larger. They're only two-bedroom homes."

"I'll talk to him now." She nodded and walked over to look at the safe. "I wanted whatever you had with your family to be safe. Do you have things that you could put in there? If not, then I can just have the extra space."

71

"I have a lot of things that should be in a safe. I've been picking up things made with my gems for decades. Silly, I know, but I sometimes marveled at the things that people did to them. When we go on a trip, I have to make myself cry, as you know. And happy tears, they make the best. I've been down in the dumps for some time, I think — not having a home did that to me. But the tears were sad, which makes for lighter colored emeralds. The same with the others. But there had been a few times when I was so thrilled with something that I laughed until I cried. I don't know if this works for you or not, but the more we produce gems, sometimes we get these little shards of them that we just eat. They don't hurt our system. But after a while, they lost their magic for us as well. We all four have shards of ourselves that we could store in there. Or you could use them."

"I might, but this will be a good place to keep them in the meantime." She walked to the drawing board that he'd only just gotten up. "I have some sketches of the log. I need a better name. Anyway, I'm going to bring them down here later, after they're all finished."

"I'd like to see it, when you're finished." He said she could come down here at any time. "I will. Also, I wanted to tell you that I'd like to someday, not right away, open a shop in town. With some of the things that the townspeople are making to make ends meet. I think, with your big name, you'll draw them in, but they might stop by other shops too. Quaint ones that will make them a few dollars. The town, I don't know if you've noticed, is starting to look better than it has before. I think that's mostly to the new mayor. Rette is doing a fantastic job, don't you think?"

"Yes, he is. And with Cassie at his side, the man is working wonders at the crime rate here too. It's the lowest it's ever been, Elissa told me." He pulled her into his arms and held her. "I love you so much, Sapphire." She said she loved him as well. "Good. Elissa wants to plan us a wedding."

Chapter 5

Melville wasn't ready to give up just yet. He wanted that woman. He'd like them both, the sapphire and the emerald, but he'd honestly take either one at this point. The thought of having an endless supply of gems like that—he'd be the richest man in the world.

"I've been out there three times, Dad. All I can see is that man." Melville asked which one. "The one that owns the house. I think his name is Blankslip or something."

"Blankenship. And he's a lord too. What the hell do you think they did to get such a title? I'd like one too." His son mumbled something under his breath, but he decided to ignore it for now. Something about title of head asshole or something. "When do you have to go to work?"

"In an hour. And so's you know, the reviews are up soon, and if I don't get better than a three, I'm out the door. Last time I skated by on a three point nine. I don't think they're going to be so generous this time." He wasn't lazy, nor was he stupid; he just had trouble reading, that was all. And no matter how many times he'd gotten him someone to help, Mel just couldn't learn the right order for his letters. "Anyway, I talked to my counselor today, and she said that she'd call them, tell them that I'm working at it. I doubt that it'll do me any good. And there are people there, these bullies, that are making it their business to make my life hellish. When are you going to go back home, Dad? You're sort of eating me out of house and home."

"You going to apply for a job that doesn't require you to read so much?" He said that he was turned down for it because he couldn't work the computer either. "I'm sorry, son. I know that you're trying very hard. As for me leaving, I told you I had three weeks of vacation coming. I'm going to use it all up for this, if I have to."

"All right. But really, you need to chip in on stuff. I don't care for going out to dinner so much. I'd rather just hang out here." If he wasn't fired from this job too. Mel was only just shy of his twenty-fifth birthday, and couldn't hold down a job for a lot of reasons. None of them were laziness nor that he didn't try, but they got sick of him asking for extra help when it came to putting products away, how to make a sign look right in a grocery store, or getting the right cart in the right space at the hospital. He was dyslexic.

Melville wasn't sure that he'd have a job when he got back either. That was why he'd put in for all his vacation now. He was sure that they were just waiting for him to screw up again before they tossed him out the door. Melville wouldn't have to work or live with his son if he could get that woman. Damn it, he hated Danburn.

It was his turn to go and watch for the women. They'd been around a great deal until he'd tipped his hand. Now he didn't have anything to go on but that he was pretty sure that they were at the lord's house. He really was going to look into that and see how that worked to get a title. He was sure that it had to do with having some money. Which he did not. Anyway, it was pouring down rain, so he decided to drive over and sit at the end of the gated road to the house.

It must take a great deal of money to be as rich as these men were. Even before Sapphire came around here, he knew that English had money out the wazoo. Also, the other two men that seemed to be hanging around now, Newton and Welsh, they had it as well. And they were spreading it around like they had an endless supply of it. He supposed that had a lot to do with the women. If he could shit emeralds every time a bill came due, he'd never have to worry about his electric being shut off nor his car being out of gas all the time, he thought with a grimace.

"What to do to get her in my grip?" He had heard all the rumors that the men were dragons. Melville had been one once. It had been a flux in the magic that he was getting and it had felt amazing. But it had only happened once, and it wasn't enough. The witch that had helped him with the deed was sadly dead. In his happiness at being something so large and menacing looking, he'd accidently stepped on her. Melville didn't *not* believe that there were some around, but whether or not these men were them, he wasn't so sure. They were old, yes, very old, but then so was he.

He'd been around enough shifters to know several things. One, never let them touch you. Well, he'd screwed that one up when Danburn threw him across the room already. Or anything that you used you took with you when you left. It was why he never drank from a glass, and why he brought his own silverware to a restaurant. Sure, he got looks, but he didn't care. Playing up the eccentric old man was what legends were made of, he thought.

Second was blood. He supposed that sort of went along with the first one, but blood was a done deal with shifters. Once they got even the littlest taste of you, they could find you in their sleep. Also, a rumor, but he believed that one. He'd seen a wolf track a woman all the way through a flooded creek bed to bring her home to her parents. Even drowned like she was, he'd found her.

Third was never promise something to any of the shifter breeds that you couldn't deliver on. He'd never had it happen to him, but he knew that they could be vindictive when they were double crossed. A friend of his had tried to run a scam on the local wolf pack, and hadn't been heard from since. It was like he'd never existed. Even his place had been cleaned out of all his things. That kind of finality was scary as fuck to him.

After several hours of nothing, not even a mail man to pass the time with, he went home. This was really getting bad. Not only did the women disappear right under his nose, but he couldn't find Danburn either. Like he'd gone to earth, as they called it, and was never going to return. But he'd have to sooner or later or there would be trouble with things. He didn't know what, but he was sure that the town was run by him, and they'd screw up without him around, he'd bet.

Mel was sitting in the kitchen drinking a cup of tea when he got home. The coffee had run out two days ago, and since Mel didn't drink it, he said that he wasn't buying it. Little did Mel know that he was paying for a great many things that he didn't know about or want.

78

"Dad, look, the houses are being worked on." He went to the window to see that his son was right. They were being worked on. At least there was a large construction company truck out front. And there she was, his sapphire. He'd started out the door when he saw the pack. "That's the kind of house I'm going to buy me someday. I've been saving since I was able to work. Just a little thing that's all mine." Not paying any attention to what Mel was saying, he nearly told him that wasn't going to happen, but the wolves there on the property were killing his plans to be rich.

The wolf pack was large; he'd heard a great deal about it when he'd been doing research on the area. You did not want to fuck with the Canon wolves. And if you did, you'd better have your will filled out and filed, as well as your next of kin notified that you were stupid. In a matter of seconds after you fucked up, he'd heard, you were a dead man. Well, at least one that no longer was a problem. Like his friend that had fucked around with another pack, you were made to disappear. Pronto.

So, all he could do was wait to see if she was stupid enough to bring her sister around so that he could claim her. Of course, his paperwork was all filled out, but he'd yet to find Danburn to file it with him. But get her he would. Then.... Well, then he'd have to figure out what to do with her. After claiming her, he knew that he'd have to show good cause for keeping her. It wasn't like he was going to wed Sapphire or anything. So really, he knew that ship had sailed with the blue sapphire.

"Her mate took her as soon as we were gone." Mel asked where he would have taken her, but Melville had ignored the question for a few of his own. "Where is the other woman?

The emerald? I need her. Everyone knows that emeralds are worth more."

Melville had no idea if they were or not, but that was how he was going to spin it. That way when asked, and he was sure that someone would, he'd say he needed her because she was like a rich gem to him. And she was. Just not like they would have thought he meant.

No one knew what he was. Because of all the blackness that he held, it was difficult to pinpoint just what sort of monster he was. Melville had cultivated that over the decades to make sure that they didn't. His son, he wasn't his either. Melville had stolen him one night when the mother of the child had died given birth. Of course, he'd had a hand in that too, but his son had never asked, and he felt no reason whatsoever to tell him. It was his secret to bear, and he did so with a light heart. Had he to do it over, however, he would have let him die with his druggie mother.

Melville dabbled in the black arts. It was what had kept him alive for so long. He never took more than he needed — well, that wasn't entirely true. When he needed a boost, he would kill. Then there were the times that he needed a thrill. Those were becoming more and more a weekly thing rather than several times a year.

The people that he got the thrill from, it wasn't as if it was as bad as it sounded, he told himself — they were the ones that screamed a great deal and kept begging. He would set a trap, and if they fell into it, he figured that he was doing the world a favor by killing off the completely stupid. Like some people he had been thinking about for the last several days.

His son for one. The kid had been nice to have around — he could draw a crowd to him like nothing ever had before.

But he was getting bossy about him finding another place to live. Harping on him about his habits of watching television all through the night. He had raised him, he should be glad to have him around. And when he found out about his money, Melville was sure that was going to get him into hot water too. Ingrate.

Danburn would be the second person. To kill off Danburn would be a large feather in his hat. Not that he could put it there; he did have enemies that would go to the first dragon they saw and tell them what he'd done. Melville had even considered killing Danburn's mother. Surely as a dragon, if indeed she was one, she'd be an old and feeble one. And where was the father, if not dead? Melville decided to go for her rather than the younger man when he wanted a thrill again.

Things were progressing slowly. He didn't have the time or resources to go after the woman for a long period of time. As it was now, he only had a few weeks left of his vacation before he had to return to his job. And then once there, it would be another year before he could come back and get her. Even if he could get her. It was looking more and more like he wasn't going to this trip. But damn it, he was going to be so broke, more so than he was even now. By then she might well be mated, or worse yet, someone else might have gotten her.

"Dad?" He looked at his son and wondered what his father had looked like. His son looked nothing like him. He wouldn't, of course, but he did wonder how fucking handsome he'd been to have such a beautiful son. The mother had been beautiful too. Right up until he slashed her throat when she told him "no" about selling him the baby. Oh, to do it over again. He might well have fucked her first. "What

81

did you want to do about dinner? I wouldn't mind staying home if you're going to that diner again. They have really good food, but I'm sick of eating out. Which reminds me, you need to chip in for groceries. I've asked you that now for two days."

Lucky for Melville, his son had lived here before the girl had come here or he might well have used up all of his cash on a hotel. Instead they were eating out. Which, by his estimation, was still cheaper than the hotel would have cost him. The diner gave large portions, as well as free drinks with your order of two dinners or more. And the desserts were out of this world fantastic.

"Yes, all right. But tomorrow, we're not going there for breakfast. I have to have cash to go home on." He didn't have much left of that even. Melville had never been any good with money. Especially when it belonged to someone else. And that was about to dry up too.

Most of his peers, people that had studied the dark arts like he had, they had saved and saved their cash when they'd been around. Now that they were all dead, he figured who was going to spend their money? No one. It bought their funerals and had paid off a few bills, but they had nothing to show for being on this earth. He was going to leave behind a legacy that people for decades would talk about. Of course, he'd be there when they did. Melville planned never to die, not with an unlimited supply of cash.

Melville had been having fun while he had it. Stealing hadn't ever been something that he was really into. He would, he thought, steal whatever was out where he could get it. But he found it to be boring to take something and then have to hide it someplace so that the police or the person that he stole if from wouldn't find him. But when he had cash, which really wasn't that often, he would spend it like it was going to last forever. And then he'd be broke again, making promises to himself to spend better. But that never lasted. As soon as he had money after so long without it, he would spend it willy nilly once more.

He finally talked his son into going with him and they walked to the diner since Mel didn't live that far from it. Usually they were both so full on the way home that they'd nearly fall asleep driving even a short distance. He asked his son what he was going to get.

"I heard that the blue-plate special is pork chops. I think that's what I'm going to get. Or the pot pie." A pie as big as your head for less than four bucks. And that would include the tea that he'd drink and all the rolls he could stuff in his face. He wondered why his son never gained an ounce, either, when he was eating that sort of stuff. "What are you going to get, Dad?"

"I don't know. I was thinking the meatloaf. If it's anything like their pot roast, I'm going to be in heaven." Mel said he didn't care for meatloaf. "Why not? My goodness, son, it has all the stuff in it you like. Meat and.... Well, I don't know what else is in it, but you like meat, don't you?" As soon as they were in the restaurant, he saw a plate of chops and decided that was what he was going to get as well.

"Hey, Mel, I need for you to do something for me." He asked him what that might be as he munched on the bread after they were seated. "I need you to try and get this girl to go out with you. She's beautiful and nice. Not super sweet, but nice when she wants to be. Why don't you ask her out, so I can take her?"

"This woman you've been calling a ball buster for a week now? You want me to date her?" Mel laughed. "I love you, Dad, but I'm so not going there. I'm not a ball buster sort of man. She'd break me if I asked her out. Not to mention, I don't date all that much, and getting a Friday night off from work is impossible. No, I don't think so."

"Why would you think something like that?" He only cocked a brow at him. "You're a good-looking man. You have a job. A car. Money in the bank." Well, he did until Melville was given access to his accounts. "Ask her out and I'll do the rest."

"She'll kill me if she found out that I lured her to you, and not think a thing about it. You said she was a dragon. How do you know that she won't burn me to a crisp and then walk away like nothing happened? Why the hell would you even think that I'd be able to pull it off?" He repeated what he'd just told him. "Dad, good looks and money do not buy a woman such as her to like you. You need to be savage and funny. Have intelligence and a wit to banter with her. I have not one of those things. I don't even know why you'd think it would work. Or for that matter, why you're bothering with this at all. Mr. English said to back off, and I think you should."

"Because I'm getting desperate. And believe it or not, not everyone listens to every word that comes out of his mouth." He was too, getting desperate, he realized. In a few days his son was going to figure out that he'd overdrawn his account, and then he'd have to explain what he'd done. It took money to get money. And the horses didn't pay off every time he made a bet. Sadly. "At least think about it. You might be my only ticket to getting close to this woman."

"No thanks. But don't say that I didn't warn you about this.

She's a beautiful woman who would turn me down as sure as shit." Even with that answer he knew that his son would do it. He was already in a better mood. Melville grabbed one of the rolls before Mel ate them all. "Besides, maybe she and I will suit and I can give you the grandkids you've always wanted."

Never, he wanted to tell his son. Never did he ever utter the words, "I'd love to be a grandfather." That was for old men and women. A thing to pass the time of the day and to have back spasms and hurt feelings. Nope, not him. He never wanted to hold another child for as long as he was on this earth. And he figured that he had a very long time to go yet.

Children were for saps, and he certainly wasn't one of those. He might be down, but he wasn't out, not yet. There was always some way for him to make a buck or two before the big one hit. He just wished the big one would hurry up and get here—he was sick of the dry spell he was in.

~~~

Sapphire knew they were never going to go for this idea. But she did promise that she'd ask. Sebastian had actually thought of the plan, and she had thought he was joking. But the more she thought about it, the better she liked it. And going to Carmine hadn't been her idea, but the little girl had been sitting quietly on the sofa when Sebastian had asked her.

"There's some trouble at school." That wasn't the way to start that conversation, Sapphire knew that, but she wanted to get things out where they could understand. Danburn asked her what was going on. "Carmine's not sure who she is. How she fits into her own family."

Quinn and Hanson were there, as well as Rette and Cassie. They'd had a family dinner tonight, but the other two, Kip and Griffith, had begged off, saying that while it was dark out, raining, they wanted to fly. Sapphire looked over at Elissa when she said that she'd heard too.

"They're teasing her, Quinn. She's not your daughter, not his child, and she isn't sure what the baby will be to her either. Stepsister, half? And then there is the mother/daughter tea coming up. They're making it hard on her to figure out who is to go with her." Sapphire told Elissa she had a plan. "Oh, my dear, I know that it'll be a good one too."

"Let Sebastian take her." No one said a word but their faces said plenty. Sapphire continued before they could tell her no. "Hear me out. He said that he's unique and that he'd stand out like a beautiful woman. But also, he's dangerous and would know how to fight. Sebastian thinks that it will give her the confidence that she needs, and she will be much better afterwards. She's suffering needlessly, and he wants to fix it for her. He's sure that he can."

"What's he going to do, kill the other children?" They were joking, but that's just what he wanted to do, she told Hanson. "No, then. He's not going to—"

"He won't. Sebastian loves her like his own child. He'd never harm her or any other child. But he hates that she cannot have a good time because her home life is so different than the other children's lives. And while she's happy at home, confused but happy, she's still different than them in a lot of ways; you knew she would be going in. And because of that, she's a target for all kinds of jokes and such." Hanson asked how having a gryphon would change that. "When you were going to show and tell at school, who was the coolest kid that day? It wasn't the kid that brought in his mom, was it? I'm betting it was someone that was very different than what you had at home."

"The kid whose father was an undertaker." Danburn laughed as the memory was told by him. "He dealt with the dead. Not that any of us had seen a dead person by then in our lives, but we knew they were around. And when he told us how he had to prepare the body for viewing, you could have heard a pin drop in the room we were so interested."

"You think that Sebastian will make it so that she's the cool kid? I mean, yes, that'll be good for one day, but what about the rest of the days? She's trying so hard." Sapphire agreed with Quinn. "I don't know about this."

"He wants to walk her to school every day. Even the cold days in winter." Kendrick asked why that was important. "Did you know that he can fly? That he can also kill someone that comes for her? And you know as well as the rest of us that she is being searched for."

"Yes, but.... Oh, I see. You think that if he's with her, she'll stand a better chance of not being hurt." Sapphire said that's not what she meant at all. "Then I don't understand."

"Carmine can take care of herself. Even under threat of being shot, I'm betting that she could bend a bullet around so that it never touched her. Each of us have given her a part of ourselves. My sisters included. Sebastian would be a distraction for her. Someone that could outrun a bullet so that she could use her considerable powers on some ass hat that wants her to come to some lab with him."

"And the flying part you talked about, that too would be a distraction for her to work her magic?" She nodded at Elissa. "I love the idea. Not just so she can get through this tea thing, but also that she gets someone with her at all times to make sure that she's safe."

"When is the tea?" Sapphire told Quinn that it was on

Friday. "All right then, he can go. Wait; why is he only going on that day?"

"To make sure that the children aren't afraid of him. He's a beautiful creature to all of us. But to a child, he might be too big, too scary for them. Also, I don't want his feelings hurt if they reject him every day." Elissa nodded as if she understood that more than others. "If you give him permission, he'll take her to the tea on Friday and bring her home. After that, we'll see how they react."

"What does Shawn say?" She was surprised that the question wasn't asked from Danburn before this. "As pack leader, he'd have to okay this. It might be what she needs, but he'd be the one that would have all the questions put to him when Sebastian leaves for the day."

"He is thrilled to have such a creature coming to his school, and will be there as well. He wishes to be there to see the kids' reaction to something so different than themselves. Also, in the future, I have made arrangements with him to have a faerie come in and talk to them about keeping the forest cleaned up, as well as a brownie to talk to them about how things are made by them." Danburn thanked her. "I didn't want to come here about this without having all the information. Also, there is one more thing that I need to ask of you all."

"Anything you want, it's yours for helping our daughter." The rest of the room agreed with Hanson and she smiled. "Within reason, I should say. I always forget to say that part when I'm happy."

"There is nothing to fear from me, I promise. I would like to talk to you about having a garden patch work." Danburn asked what that was, but Elissa knew and told him. "You mean have a garden patch set up for the townspeople to use? We tried that once before and it became a disaster. People were stealing another person's food. There wasn't anything to keep the animals out of the gardens, and they lost a great deal on that. The only thing that came out on top was the deer."

"I've a different approach. There will be vegetable and fruits assignments. People will be responsible for growing, say, green beans. And someone else will be growing peas. They can work together if they wish, but one person will be assigned something to grow. Once the produce starts to come on, they can barter their goods for someone else's. Say the potato man would like some green peas. Then he would barter for them with his things. It has worked before when there was enough equipment to make the job easier."

"You mean to buy a tiller, or even hoes and such." She told him that sometimes it would be the only thing keeping the gardener from being able to do his garden correctly. And having the right equipment would make it easier for all of them. "Who will be in charge of this? To be honest, I have too much on my plate as it is. I would love to help, but I just can't."

"Mr. Crocket said that he'd help. In fact, this was entirely his idea. He said that it would help him, what with his job now in watching over our lands, to have someone play around in the dirt for him. That's another thing, it would be a family thing. And no cell phones would be allowed within two yards of the garden area. I can take care that there is no service around the plots to ensure that it doesn't happen." He laughed and asked how that would go over. "I don't care. This will be family time, as I said. And between the hours of whatever time frame we decide, the cell service in the town

89

will be turned off too. Family time."

"What do you think, Danburn?" She loved Elissa, but right now she wasn't sure that she still agreed with her on the plan. "I mean, it sounds like a solid plan. And you were just saying the other day how you'd like to see more involvement around the town. Perhaps this might be a start. And the fact that you'd not have to oversee it, that should be a good thing for you, wouldn't you think?"

"There is more, if you want to know." Danburn nodded and Sapphire pulled her notes from her pocket. "Mr. Crocket said that he and his sons would like a hand in reopening the greenhouse. It's too late for this year, but they think, with a little help and a loan, they can get it running by fall for Christmas. I've spoken to Dana about it, and he and I are going to give them the loan to start it. But like a good dragon, I'm asking you for permission. Not that I need it, really." She grinned at Danburn.

"Christmas? Why so late in the year? And what does he plan to sell in the winter?" Danburn looked at his mom when she told him to hush and listen. "Mom, the ground is frozen solid that time of year. You couldn't plant a thing the way the weather is around here. Cold as a witch tit in a brass brassiere one day and hotter than Hades the next."

She popped him in the back of the head. "There is no reason for you to be vulgar, Danburn." Elissa looked at Sapphire with a smile. "Go on dear, ignore the bad man for now."

"Yes, but there are things that can be sold in the fall. Foliage for one thing. Trees in the fall. From what I've seen on the outlaying properties, there once was a grove of pine trees that have been all but forgotten. Mr. Crocket said that you

could get the land cleared and make some cash on the side."
Danburn perked up but didn't say anything. "Also, there are
the school children. They can come in in early spring and
plant something for their mothers for Mother's Day. Trees can
be planted as well. And spring flowers are a huge hit when
there has been snow on the ground for months."

"This Crocket person seems to be stretching himself pretty
thin. What's going to happen to all these projects if he can't
get to all of them when someone needs him?" It was a fair
question and one she had an answer to. Instead of answering
him, she handed him the list. "What's this?"

"Those are the names of the people that have been
assigned to each project, should you approve. And even if
you don't, Dana and I are going to make sure that some of
them are started, for the good of the community." He looked
at her hard. "It's a good thing, Danburn. A lot of these people
have been out of work for a very long time. And like Mr.
Crocket, they only need a hand up to get their homes in order.
Kids to the dentist. A car that runs every time they start it
and not only in the warmer weather. There is a list of over
two hundred people, most of them pack but a lot of humans
too. Like Carmine, they need to have just a little boost to their
hearts to get themselves feeling like they can do just about
anything."

"You've put a great deal of work into this." She said that
it had been easy with Mr. Crocket's help. "This man, he works
for you? Or do you have him already working on some of
these projects?"

"He's going to get his sons started on their project at the
greenhouse when you approve it. They're so sure of this that
two of his sons are quitting their jobs to devote to it full time.

The garden project is already started, you might as well know. That's going to be his baby, so to speak." Danburn looked at her for a full minute before he burst into laughter. "I can't wait all day on you to approve something that I know will work. Sir."

"Yes, well, that sir at the end isn't necessary. You did a great job, and I'll approve of all of it. And fund them. For a start. After the first...let's say five years, then they'll have to show some kind of profit on the ones that can. But the garden project is the best idea I've heard. If you can keep it working."

"I will." She knew she would too. Or heads would roll. Not really, she thought to herself, but she would keep them going if she had to help them herself. Help, not do. That's what Dana had told her from the very start. "Thanks, Danburn. I didn't know what to expect, but I thank you for this. You've made a great many people happy. And in doing this, you've put some food on their tables that they can take pride in too."

"I might even have a little of the produce myself. And if you can get a few in the orchard in the back to help with picking, I'll give them a decent wage and one quarter of what they pick from the trees." She said that they were already working on their trees. "I think they were planted at the same time, so if you need to replace, I'm sure we will too. It all bears looking into now."

"That's very generous of you. And I thank you again." He said that he had to do something better than she could. "Oh, we did the same; they're getting half the profits they show for each year they're ahead, and they have the option of paying the loan off early. But we've cautioned them on that move. For now."

He was still laughing when lunch was called for them.

Sapphire was beginning to like the big dragon. And she decided that since her sisters were missing so much being hidden away, she'd start a diary so that they could at least be able to keep up with the goings on that were happening in their new homes. Also, they'd be able to not be behind on the projects that were being started. It would be as if they had never left.

Chapter 6

Dana was working on the log piece when he felt someone in the room with him. He didn't so much as look around, letting Dragon do it for him. He told him that it was the man that wanted his mate. Laying down his tools, he turned to look at the man.

"You're trespassing, Melville. And I thought you were told not to come on this property again." Melville just waved him off. "I have a feeling that you're going to get yourself killed. And soon. Is there anyone that I can contact for you?"

"I want the sister. Since you've claimed the one I want, you must hand over the sister. It's only fair, don't you think?" Dana said nothing. "You're not being reasonable, you know that, don't you? I mean, for all you know she could be my son's mate, and then I would have her anyway."

"What are you?" He didn't use compulsion this time, but he would if he didn't get any answers. "You're not at all what we thought. Immortal? Yes. You have been around for I would say.... You're about a couple hundred years old. Give or take a decade. A monster? Yes, we've discovered that as well. What are you?"

"I'm one hundred and forty-two years old, as a matter of fact, but that is neither here nor there. I want the woman. I need her for my…. What difference does it make? I just need her." Dana wasn't finished with his questions yet, and asked him what he was again. "At one time I was a great human."

"I highly doubt that you were anything that even was mildly great. Perhaps you've changed your memory to suit yourself. I'd say you were a trash picker. You know what that is, don't you? Someone that has to go to the dump daily to find a bit of this or that. And you have a child, too. Mel isn't yours. How on earth did you manage that?"

Dragon spoke again. *He has stolen the child that he claims. While the mother lay dying, he cut her throat and took the child before its first breath. He is surely disappointed in the child that is now a man, but he loves what the child can give to him despite his disabilities.*

"So you'll even stoop so low as to take a child that doesn't belong to you and kill the dying mother while at it." The man looked shocked, but Dragon wasn't through feeding him information. "You've done a lot of nasty things over the years, haven't you, Melville? And the title that you so freely throw about, it's about as real as the name that you now use. Isn't that right, Robert of the widow? Your poor mother. Did she ever find out that you killed her husband? Or that you made it so that she'd fall down the stairs and abort your poor brother? How about the fact that you've — ?"

"Enough. Lies, all of it. Where did you get such lies about me? I demand that you tell me right now. This isn't very nice of you to throw them at me as if they're true." He tried to laugh it off, but all he did was make himself look guiltier. "What is it you hope to gain, young man? I'm sure that you've done some things that you're not proud of either. Had I known that we were going to throw accusations at each other, I might have been better prepared."

"Perhaps I do have skeletons in my closet. But the difference is, I've made myself a better man. You, over the years, have not. What is it you think to do with my sister-in-law? Drain her? That won't work, you know. You cannot drain a dragon like her." He asked what he meant. "She's a very special dragon, as is my mate. You cannot capture her and make her into your own little bank without consequences. Like the dragon council. Did you know that they have special cells for men just like you?"

"You lie." He said that he didn't. "Then you exaggerate. Which is the same thing, you know. Where is she? I have demanded that you bring her to me, and I want it done now. I don't want to be here any more than you wish for me to be. Just bring the girl and I'll be on my way."

"I have sent her away." Melville actually stomped his foot at him. "You're such a child. And by the way, I'm much older than I look, and thousands of years older than you are. I have powers that will make your little bit of black magic look like a small child's science project. And if you continue to piss me off, I'll show you just how much I have."

"What sort of powers do you have? None, I tell you. So? You have a bit of information on me. That means nothing. It's all lies anyway. You have it that I might have killed my father. He is long since turned to dust, and there's no proof of the deed anyway. My title? I'm sure there are millions of people doing the same thing as I and getting better results.

Maybe you have done the same, for all I know. You might be the trash picker you accused me of being, since you have so many details about the job. As for the child? Some would say that I saved his life with I took him from his druggie mother. Others, like you, say that I don't deserve him. What do you think would have become of him if I didn't take him? *If* I took him."

Dana wanted to show him his dragon, but knew that would be a mistake. He was covered in diamonds, his body harder than most that he knew. So he only snapped his fingers and watched as Melville dropped to the floor, his body pinned there by nothing more than magic. Dana moved to kneel over the man.

"No magic? Right now I could strip you of your flesh and have a meal of it. I could take out your eyes without a single drop of blood marring my office. There are many things that I could do to you, Melville, all of which you'd not be able to do a damned thing about. Shall I show you?" He blinked several times, his mouth no longer working either. When he heard his name said softly, he turned and looked at his beautiful mate. "Hello, my love. Melville here was telling me that I have no magic to speak of, and that I lie all the time. What shall I do with him?"

"Carmine called me. She said for you to let him go. His son needs him." Dana stood up and so did Melville. He might not care for the man, but he wouldn't keep him from his son. "Go now before I tell him to finish the job."

Melville disappeared and she came to him. Asking her what had happened to the son, she just looked up at him and smiled. It was a ruse.

"You little devil, you. Why did I not see what a minx you

are?" She said that Carmine had called, but she had said that he needed to be let go. "Did she say why?"

"No. She said that she'd not been able to see that. Only that he had to be free for some reason. And it was important." Dana trusted Carmine because she hadn't been wrong about anything as yet. "The school thing is today. I'm sort of nervous for them both. But Sebastian is very excited, and so is Carmine."

"Good. I have to get my animal today too, then?" She told him they were here. "Before I do this, tell me why I need one. I mean, Dragon speaks to me now. And he can do some pretty amazing things for me."

"Yes, but can he go and search things for you? Sebastian, for what he is, can run a computer. He's very strong too. Like move a wall of concrete should I be trapped. It's happened to us before when we were planting the gems." He nodded. "You want to pick the one that calls to you. And she will. Just let her come to you and you'll be paired with her."

"What is it that she'll do for me other than walls? And I'm not kidding you, I've been trapped before and my dragon couldn't be brought out because of the iron shackles that were around me." She said that she'd be able to take the iron off him. "Okay. All right then. Let's get this done. The safer we can both be, the better I'll feel."

They assembled in the room with them. There were a varied and odd sort of group. There were things here that he'd not seen in a long while, nor had he ever seen in all his life. But they all seemed to know which one not only called to him, but seemed to need him to take her. The succubus.

"I am unlike the others, my lord. I will, because of what I am, need to be a part of your body. And that of your mate. Men

99

will...I am too magical to be left in the world of men." Dana nodded; he could see that. She was indeed very beautiful. "Not just my beauty, my lord, but what I am as well. Do you know the story of a succubus?"

"You are said to have sex with sleeping men. I have no reason to believe that one way or the other, but I want you to know, you're never to touch me." She nodded and bowed before him. It was then that he noticed that the others were gone. "You are my counterpart then."

"Yes, my lord." He told her to call him Dana. "I cannot. That would be familiar, and I cannot be that with you." She looked at Sapphire, then back at him. "I am a succubus. My name is Ferne. That is all, the only name I have ever had."

"How do you come to my body then? And you said that you'd be with us both. How does that work?" She came to him and he could feel her magic; it was like he was being bathed in it. Then almost as suddenly as he could smell her, he couldn't any longer. "Ferne, did you do that?"

"Nay, my lord. You have my scent now, and then it was gone for you. You will only need it again to find me should something happen." He nodded, and when she smiled at him, he smiled back. "Put out your hands, please? I shall show you what I do to come to you."

He did as was asked and her long sharp nails ran over his palm, as they did Sapphire's. Blood welled up then it was gone, as was Ferne. But he felt her on his belly and lifted his shirt.

She was there, climbing up his belly to his chest like a person would a rock wall. Her nails were sticking in him, but they weren't as painful as he'd thought them to be. When she turned and looked at him, as if she were asking him if he was finished, he put his shirt down and looked at Sapphire.

"She's on my back. I'm assuming that's where she was headed on you." Dana was slightly freaked out and told Sapphire that. "Don't be. I'm glad that you have someone to help you. And me, I suppose. Succubi are very strong."

"I never thought that this would be in my realm of things happening to me today." She laughed with him. "Not to mention, I have this being on my back that moves around. I hope she's still when I'm working. I can't handle any more distractions."

He showed her what he was working on before he had a visitor. Then he told her what Melville had wanted. The man was going to be in serious trouble if he didn't chill out and behave himself. The knowledge that he'd killed that woman over the child wasn't going to sit well with a great many people.

"Melville wants your sister. I told him that she was gone, that I had sent her away. But he said something that got me to thinking. What if her mate is here? And that by keeping them like they are, they'll not meet." Sapphire told him that if he was here, then it was meant to be that he'd wait on her too. "I hope so. I'd hate to be responsible for someone not feeling like I do having you around."

"There won't be a meeting if she's hurt badly. And who did he have in mind? I'm sure it's that son of his." Dana nodded and laughed. "I will not allow her to be mated to that man's son."

"It's not his son." He explained to her what Dragon had told him. "I was going to see if I could find out something about the mother and the boy. For all we know, she might have died anyway, but maybe not. If he cut her throat and

101

she wasn't a druggie, but say a diabetic that might have been having a problem, then we can get him on murder. I'll have Dragon or even Ferne try and find out what they can about her death. Right now, I want her to be a druggie, but also, I'd like to see him arrested for his crimes. Not that killing a druggie is better. But if she wasn't, that means that family is out there wondering what happened to their baby boy."

"We'd need to know where it happened and about the time frame." Dragon told him and then Dana told Sapphire. "All right. I'll ask your sister to look. Kendrick seems to have an uncanny ability to get to the bottom of things quickly. Oh, and my projects have been approved. I'm going to go and tell Denny now. He'll be so happy. Not that we weren't going to do them anyway, but this way I don't have to tell him I'm sorry when he figures it out."

When she left him, after a very consuming kiss and a promise to be careful, he went back to work. He loved this project and was excited to see it finished. Looking at the log of clay that he'd built up around a wire mesh, he decided that he'd done the best he could and now it had to dry. If he tinkered with it too much, it would never look right. Done was done, and he had to walk away from it. Once it was dry, he would cut it in half lengthwise and then let it dry some more. When it was ready, he'd make a plaster mold of both sides separately by putting the clay directly in boxes and pouring plaster around it. A few days after that, when the plaster was as dry as it could be, he'd pour in the pewter and fill in all the nooks and crannies to make sure that it was just the way he wanted it. Pouring out the extra pewter, he would let it set.

That would take only a few hours, but he was going to give it a few days. Just to be sure that some of the thicker parts, such as the grain of the wood, was perfect. To remove the pewter from the mold, he'd have to break the plaster away. Then clean it all from the mold.

Before he was to make the mold of pewter, however, he'd make a rubber negative of the mold. By pouring rubber, a lot like the soles of shoes is made of, in the plaster molds, he'd have a copy of the work so that he could make another mold of plaster when he needed it. That way, he could make another log if he wanted to make more of them for another project. He looked around the small room that he was working in to keep the dust to a minimum, and was pleased that things were going so well here.

While that all set up, he started forming the little creatures that would be a part of the piece when he was finished cleaning it. Looking at the little faerie that he was working on, he thought about the shape of the gems he was going to use to make her wings. Excitement drew him in as he worked until his back hurt.

~~~

Sapphire saw the younger man before he did her. He looked so sad that she wasn't sure that she could yell at him for being where he was unwelcome. She might not know his name, but she could smell Melville all over him. And when he looked up, she saw the black eye and busted lip that he had.

"What happened to you? You're bleeding badly on your forehead. Come with me so I can fix you up." She grabbed him by the arm and took him into the nursery they were working on for spring planting. "Who hit you? Your father? So help me, I'll tear him apart if he did this to you. No one needs to be hitting their children, I don't—"

The man, she could see that now, grabbed her hand and

held it. She smiled down at him when he did to her. Backing away from him, she let him explain when he requested to do so.

"I got this from work. Not my dad. But he's not going to be happy with me when I tell him about being fired. We need...I need the job for money." She asked him what he'd done at work to get himself fired. "I'm dyslexic. Letters are hard enough, but numbers really mess things up. I work... worked in a warehouse. And when I put an entire truck of stuff away in the wrong places, the guy that had to move them all beat me up. I think he was madder at me then the boss was."

"What's his name?" He said he wasn't telling her, she was just too scary. "Probably a good thing. But I am going to clean you up a bit. I don't think you need stitches, but I can tape your lip closed. Here you go, just sit still."

He did just what she asked him to do while she cleaned the wounds. While she was doing that, she found out the name of the three people that had beaten him up. Three men against one wasn't going to cut it with her, and she was going to make sure that they learned the error of their ways.

They had waited outside when he left to do this to him, calling him names while they were at it. She wasn't surprised to figure out that the name calling hurt the boy more than the beating did. She also found out that he was the most gentle, loving person that she'd ever encountered. Despite the man who had raised him.

"I have a job for you if you want it." He told her who he was. "I know who you are. Not your name, but who you're related to. I don't care for Melville, not at all, but you're not like him. And the job offer still stands. If you can work with

Mr. Crocket."

"Denny? Yes, I've worked for him before. When he had some people trash up his house, me and him, we painted all the dirty words off his house before his wife came home from the store. Did you know that he doesn't have much money?" She said that he did now. "He's a nice man. But yes, I can work with him. He...he kinda gets what's wrong with me and writes it all down so I can figure it out. It helps me."

"Well, he's going to start working for me when we get the greenhouse up and running. But first it needs to be cleaned up. And if you want the job, you'll work with his boys in the nursery here. We're going to grow plants for the gardens that we're putting in." He said that he'd like that too. "You'll have to let him explain it to you. He has a list of people that want to help out. Mel, you go and talk to him about it, and if he wants to hire you, then you'll report to him. But I won't have you trying to get my sisters for your dad."

"No, I won't. He's kinda set on that. But he'll be leaving soon anyway, or he'll lose his job. If he hasn't already. Dad was supposed to return last Monday, but he didn't. Told them he was sick or something like that." Mel seemed torn about something and looked at her. "You're very pretty. And I bet your sisters are too. Don't let him have you guys, Miss Sapphire. If he gets you he'll ruin you. I've seen his handy work before. It's why I moved here, to get away from him for a bit."

When she sent him to find Denny, she looked at what needed to be done in the office. There was a lot of mess, that was for sure. And very little in the way of electrical outlets. That was going to have to be taken care of first and foremost. Instead of waiting on someone to come and do it,

Sapphire used a bit of her own magic to make the office not just cleaned up, but also manageable for a computer and all the office equipment that she'd need. She needed just one place that she could go to while here that wasn't torn apart, molded, or rotten. The greenhouse was a total mess but for the greenhouse itself.

By lunch time Sapphire hadn't heard from Denny nor Mel. Figuring that they were getting along all right, she went to find them to see about lunch. It hadn't occurred to her until then that both of them might not have the funds for such a treat. When she found them, Sapphire paused when she heard the two of them talking.

"You do this up right, Mel, and I might have you working right under me as my right-hand man. I never was very good at fixing things like this." Mel said something about it being easy for him, and that made Denny laugh. "Yes, but don't you be calling yourself a retard. I don't care if you think it's funny that a man like you can fix things. You're not that. You got something wrong in your head, that's all. Don't make you a dummy."

"All right, Denny. Turn on the water and let's see if I fixed it or not."

She watched as the water was turned on and the water shot through the hoses that were hanging from the ceiling of the greenhouse. When they were satisfied with it, she walked in just as the water was turned off.

"How about some lunch? My treat." They both nodded eagerly. "I saw that you got the water running. That should save us a bundle."

"I didn't do nothing more than turn on the water, miss. It was all Mel here. I'm telling you, if it's got parts, he can

106

surely fix it if it's not working. And while he might not know the names of the pieces, he can break them down so that you can order them. The kid is a wizard at anything with moving parts, I tell you."

She liked that Denny didn't take credit, and that Mel was blushing like she'd asked him to kiss her. She was going to enjoy working with these two men. And she was going to enjoy watching Mel come into his own. She had a feeling that few people had done much for him, including his father.

"I have set up a line of credit for you at the hardware store. I know you have a list of things that you need." He said that he did but wanted to know his limit. "There isn't one. I trust you. And before I forget, Danburn and his wife donated three rototillers, a large tractor that needs just one or two people to drive it, as well as an open trailer so that things can be hauled around in it. You also have some yard equipment. I don't know what all there is, but have a look at it before you go and see if you need anything else. Oh, and a truck. I've put your information on the insurance, Denny. If you trust Mel's driving, then I can have him added as well. All I ask is that you be careful with it. Its new, and I know nothing about driving."

"You don't know how to drive?" She told Mel that she'd never had an occasion to learn. "I can see that and all, you having wings, but driving is fun. Just to be able to get out and let the air run through your hair and all."

"Thank you, but I think I'll stick to flying. That way I won't run someone off the road or get stuck in a ditch with a tire all messed up." They both laughed with her. "All right, gentlemen, I'll go and get lunch, then you guys can go and see about getting what we need to clean up here, and with the garden project too."

She hadn't been sure that Mel knew what she was. Denny was a wolf, and he wasn't even a full-blooded one. But Sapphire supposed that in the long run it was better that Mel knew, and she'd have to watch that his dad didn't try to exploit her newest employee. She was going to watch him like a mother hen from now on.

The rest of the afternoon she worked on separating out the trash from the usable. She wasn't one to waste anything if she didn't have to. When the two of them returned from town, she could tell that it hadn't gone as well as she had hoped. Mel was really upset, and she had a feeling that it was about his father and not the trip.

"He wanted Mel to tell him where you were. Told him right off that he wasn't going to do it, that you'd fixed him up. Wasn't even sure that he meant the lip or the job, but his dad didn't like it either way. Then he wanted him to pay for some things that he wanted to return. Didn't get that either until Mel told me that you'd be charged for the stuff, then he'd bring it back in a week for the cash. You'd never know, he thought. Well, Mel told him right off he wasn't ever going to do that. I got a whiff of him now — he's not going to be coming around here without me knowing it." She asked Denny if Mel had been hurt. "Nah, just his feelings, and those will mend, I think. Doesn't seem to me that he gets much loving in the form of his dad none. Told me on the way back here that nobody had done a better clean up job on him than you had, and you ain't even his mom."

She went to find Mel when Denny told her about his bank account too. He'd tried to buy himself a soda, not getting those much now that his daddy was there. But his account was overdrawn and he owed it money. Apparently, Melville had sweet talked a woman at the bank into give him a copy of Mel's card, saying that Mel had approved so he'd have pocket money while he was there. Mel was really hurt about that.

"Mel? Denny told me about your dad. And what happened at the bank and hardware store." She saw him nod, but he wouldn't turn around. "I can help you get your money back if you'd like."

"Nah, it's gone. I just wanted me a pop, you know? Like a working man can have one." She made a mental note to get a fridge for here with sodas in it. "He took out all my savings, Miss Sapphire. Every penny I saved up. Over six hundred dollars. And you can bet that as soon as I put more money in there, if I do, he'll take that too. Why would he do that to me? I worked really hard for that money. And here I thought while he was here, it was his money he was spending because I gave him a place to stay. Did you know that he even took my bed, had me sleeping on the couch? I guess he's a lot like some people said. A liar and a thief."

She wanted to tell him that his dad was a dick, but didn't. Instead, she offered to help him set up another account at the bank, and to spot him the money to pay off the other one. It took her an hour but, in the end, he finally gave in and went with her to the bank. The sooner they got this taken care of the better things would be for Mel. And Melville was going to pay too.

"I'm sorry about this, Mel. I didn't know who was taking the money out; he used your card." Mel told the banker that he'd left it out and then couldn't find it after a while, and didn't mention about the other woman who had given Melville the card. Sapphire would, when she came back. The woman had been the reason that he'd gotten into his bank account in the first place. "Yes, well, might I suggest, at least for the time being, that you keep it on your person. We could set it up so that you can only use it with a proper identification. Such as when you go to the store and such. It won't work on the ATM out front, however, but that's not such a bad thing, is it?"

"Yes, sir, I think that's a wonderful idea. And he won't get it again. I'll make sure of it." He sounded so strong in that moment that she knew that Melville wouldn't get it without a fight. She almost felt sorry for Melville. But not enough to warn him. He would get what he deserved if he messed with the boy.

It took them only a few minutes to get it squared away. After putting the money in the account to bring it to zero, the banker waived half the fees he'd been charged because they'd sort of let him get by with it too. Sapphire lent Mel another five hundred to get him food for himself, and she even bought him a soda on the way home. It was, after that, a pretty good day, she thought. It was a lot of money to give to a new employee, but she needed to do something. So much was like Carmine and her trip to school lately. She wondered if the fates were making sure that they were sticking together on things like this.

"I'm gonna have to ask him to go home. And if that doesn't work, I'm going to tell him he has to go home. I don't want him hanging around anymore." She was glad and told him that. "Yeah, he's not helping me out any, and when he's there, I can't watch my television shows and he messes with my things. I like them just so. Then there is the added fact that he took my hard-earned money, making me believe that it was his when it wasn't."

"I know how you feel about things being just so. When I'm working, that's the way I like them as well. Where is it you live?" He told her across from the little houses that were being worked on.

"It's a tiny little apartment, not big enough for the two of us. And there ain't much in the way of towels and stuff for the both of us either. Dad don't even clean up the kitchen. I do think the tiny fridge and stove are cute, but they don't make Dad happy none. He complains about everything I have." Mel snorted. "I'd sure like to have been able to buy me a house. That's what I was saving for. A house is nicer than an apartment any old day. Plus, you have a yard to mow. I think that would be about the greatest thing, to mow my own lawn."

"Mel, I have an idea. Did you want to live in one of the houses? We're going to offer them up to people who work for us for a cut rate." It was a fib—they were going to rent them out to anyone that wanted them. "The first one is about done. It was the easiest to fix. And all the kitchen appliances are full sized too. The one I'm talking about, it has three bedrooms, and I know that's a little large for you, but you could use one as an office and one as a gaming room."

"Really? Heck, I'd like that. What's the rent?" He told her what he'd been paying at the apartment, which to her was a lot more than it was worth. "I can't do no better than that until I get my feet back under me."

"You kick your dad to the curb and you can live there for free for one year. So long as you work for me in that year." He put out his hand and she took it. "Good deal. You go home, kick your father out, pack up, and then we'll see you at the greenhouse in the morning."

111

Chapter 7

Elissa loved the new shop that dealt in T-shirts and tied dyed things. She had picked out four for herself before she heard someone talking about shirts for his business. And then there was the man behind him that wanted to know the cost for tees for the local baseball teams. He said he was looking for sponsors. Her mind went crazy trying to figure out how she could make it work for them all. Just do it, she thought, and smiled as she made her way to the back of the store to the counter. Both men tipped their hats at her. The owner of the store, she didn't know his name, told her welcome to his shop.

"I'll sponsor the team and get them shirts. Also, any equipment that you need. See about getting other teams together and we'll help them out as well." Bob Martin, the coach, thanked her. "You're so very welcome. I'm glad that you're taking this on. You need anything, you let me know."

"Thank you very much, Lady Elissa. I'll tell the boys and girls." He laughed. "Your son is going to be upset that you're doing this and not allowing him to, isn't he?"

"Why do you think I jumped right on it? Anytime I can be one step ahead of him is a happy day for me." Laughing, she turned to the other man. "How did you get the design for your shirts? You help me create some for the gardeners that work for us, and I'll pay for yours as well."

"Thanks. As much as I'd like to take credit for it, I got it here. Mr. Knisley does it pretty good for a small fee." Elissa looked at the man who was blushing brightly. "I think he gets them off the computer or something. But you'd never know it to see them. They look as good as anything you'd get in one of them big stores."

It took her nearly an hour to decide on the one that she liked. And it wasn't really what she wanted. It was simple, really, much easier than coming up with a name for them. Elissa wanted to use the word dragon in it, but wasn't sure how to incorporate it into the design, then he showed her the dragon wrapped around the tree.

"Oh my yes, that's perfect. I think we should simply call it Dragon's Breath of Fresh Air, as you suggested." Again Mr. Knisley blushed brightly. "How long will it take you to do a few of them? I think we have about a dozen men working now, but I think only two of them are anyone that I'm sure of. It's going to be so wonderful to have the shirts. When we open, they'll be able to tell a worker from the customers, don't you think?"

"If you tell me their names, I'll put those on there for free. It's the least I can do for you, Lady Elissa. You brought me in a lot of work today." She even got to pick the color, and of course picked a bright green and a bright orange. Elissa even had herself printed one up, as well as Sapphire. "This is going to keep me out of the poor house, so you know. And if we can get other sponsors for the other teams for baseball, I'll cut them a good rate like I am for you. Things sure have a way of working out, don't you think, ma'am?"

"If they can't find any sponsors for the other teams, you let me or Danburn know. He might take on one or two himself. And I know that the greenhouse would love to be one as well, I'm betting. There are so many things that we can do to help our little town, don't you think?" He agreed with her and started on the shirt. "Thank you so much for this. I'm sure that Sapphire will be as tickled as I am about them."

He was serious about being broke, she knew that. But this was going to help so many people. Not just with the new jobs, but keeping the ones that were working now busy as well. As soon as he was finished with the shirts, Elissa took them to the greenhouse to hand them to Mel, Denny, and Sapphire. Elissa pulled hers over her silk blouse to wear.

"Mom? What are...? You went and got them? I wanted to do that." Danburn showed up just as she was modeling her shirt for them all. "They look fantastic, however. I love the name. Good job on that, Sapphire."

"Your mom did it all. I love it too. We'll have to get something for the truck. Oh, I have to talk to you later, Danburn, about those little houses." He told her that was fine and they walked around the building. Elissa was seeing the improvements better because she'd been here before they'd cleaned up some of it. "This is impressive. I thought it would be in worse shape than it's in."

"It was. Denny and Mel have been working on it non-stop since he got here today." When they were in the back of the building, all alone, Sapphire told Danburn what had

115

happened today and what Mel was going to do for them. "He isn't lying when he said that he's going to kick him to the curb, Danburn. You believe me, don't you?"

"Of course I do. But there is still the issue that he's his father. That will play a huge role in what he does. We'll have to make sure that we keep a close eye on him. Just to make sure that he doesn't get hurt again. I'm assuming that he did that to him?" Sapphire told him no, it was his former job, but she was looking into that as well. Then Elissa brought up the houses and the rent for the poor boy, helping Sapphire out when she was called away. "Perfect. I love that he's going to take one. And you've explained to him about not allowing his father there? We don't need any trouble from him now."

"He said he wasn't going to live with him, son. Mel wants his life to be on a better road, and he's pretty much said that his father isn't going to be helpful in that." Danburn agreed. "I think this will work out better for all of us, including Mel. And if his father comes around, the boy won't have any place to live. That's the deal Sapphire made with him. No rent for a year, and then he can save his money for a house that he wants. I think you'd do well to sell those off to the people that are going to be living in them. Sort of one of those rent to own kind of deals."

"Mom, I never thought this would get this far — the town, I mean. It's been going down so slowly that I never noticed things getting into disrepair. But now the buildings are being cleaned up along the main street. The people are walking around, eating ice cream and having a good time. I saw Mr. Kennedy out this morning watering plants in that big planter that sat out there empty for all these years. And Mr. Bash, he was sweeping the sidewalk and having a good time at it. It's been a pleasant surprise seeing the town come back together after all this time."

"I think you owe a great deal of that to Sapphire. She's been out here nearly every day working on one thing or another. I think she'd be at the houses too, but they ran her off. She was begging to be able to run the equipment." They both laughed as they made their way to the front. "I think that she's making sure to throw your name around too. She is doing that because she wants people to know that you're behind this all the way."

"I am." She told him about the T-shirts for the ball players. Danburn mentioned his drive by today. "I was just by the fields and saw that they're in poor repair. I sent out a crew to mow and get it cleaned up. There was enough trash out there that I bet we could fill a dumpster."

"Danburn, I have to tell you, I'm so excited about all this. Your father would be so proud of the little town, don't you think? And of you. He'd just love having all his boys here, as he called you and the others. And the mates. My goodness, he'd be in seventh heaven knowing that there will be a baby soon." Danburn agreed with her, and she felt better when he hugged her. "I miss him so much, but this certainly helps. Dragon's Breath is going to be a big hit, and when Sapphire gets done, you can bet the rest of the town is going to be as well."

Elissa heard them arguing even before she saw them. Melville was arguing with his son, not Sapphire, who apparently was there for support. The way she kept telling Mel to say what was in his heart was funny, if not a little scary. She didn't want anyone hurt, and was afraid it was going to come to that.

117

"You are not going to hurt me again, Dad. It's my life and my money, and I'm sick of you telling me how you're going to be rich on selling one of them women. Don't you understand that they're people? That you can't just say, hey, I'm going to sell her so I can be rich? No, you can't do that. And I'm not going to help you. In fact, I'm going to try my best to stop you." Melville said that he'd not been touched today, not yet anyway. But if he kept this bull shit up, he certainly would be. "I'm a grown man, and the sooner you realize that, the better off we'll be. But you have to tell me why. Dad, you took all my money and overdrew my account. They charged me a lot of money to close that account up to open another one. I can't keep you in cash and make my bills and stuff. You told me that you were spending your own money all this time. You never took me out those times. You weren't being generous or kind like I thought, but being a thief, taking my hard-earned money."

"Oh, stop whining. I thought you said you were a man. You're nothing unless I say so. As for your account, you closed it? Why would you do that? I mean, you'll have to open it back up soon. Or you can just give me access to the new one. That way I won't have to lie to get one. I can go and help you out with things. You have bills to pay and so on, and I can do that for you. For letting me stay with you." Mel told him that he was doing just fine before he got there, and would be doing fine after he left him. "Well, I have to tell you son, I've lost my job back home. I might be staying with you for a bit longer, I'm afraid."

"No you won't, Dad. I don't live in the apartment anymore, so this might be a good thing for you. You can take it over and live there by yourself. I'd find a job too, if I was you. They'll want you to pay the rent every month like I had to do."

His dad must have noticed them standing there, so he started acting a little put out about the arrangements.

"Do you believe this kid? I bring him into the world and raise him up to be a good man, and what does he do? Kicks me out of his home like I didn't provide for him all his life." Elissa had enough of this man. And said that he wasn't even his father. "Now, don't be lying to him. That's not right. Is it, Danburn?"

"You're not on friendly terms with me, so you will call me by my title or Mr. English. And it is true, you're no more his father than I am yours. And had you been mine, you never would have made it to puberty." Mel turned and looked at them, then back at his dad. "He's not your father, son, but a man who stole you from your mom when you were newly born."

"No, that can't be true. Dad, you said that.... You lied to me? All this time? When I asked you about what the doctor said, about us being so different, you said it was the way things went. Then when I asked you why I was so different, you told me that it was my mom's fault, that she'd done drugs when I was in her womb. Why would you do that to me?" Melville told the boy that his mother had done drugs, and that she was a whore too. "No, I won't believe you. You've lied to me enough. I'm glad that I'm not going to have to take care of you anymore. I don't want you to come around me either. I want you to leave me alone. I don't want.... You lied to me about my whole life. How could you do that to me?"

When Mel turned his back on his father and walked away, Danburn stepped in front of Melville to stop him from following the younger man. But Sapphire went after Mel, as did Denny. If anyone could help the boy, she knew that they could do it. When Melville asked him what he'd done that for, her son only laughed.

"No good is going to come from him knowing the truth. And now he's all mad at me and stuff." Melville looked in the direction that they had gone. "He didn't give me any cash either. How am I supposed to live without something to get around on? My next check won't be enough to cover my expenses and the bills that an apartment will generate."

"You didn't think he needed the truth? I do. And I have someone looking into the death of that woman you killed." He said that he'd not killed her, but she'd been dying. "But you did slit her throat and take her child, didn't you? While she was still alive. That is against the law. And it doesn't matter if she was dying already or on drugs, she died because of your actions that day. Then you took her child. You don't think someone out there might have wanted him?"

"No one will give a shit about a druggie woman so high on shit that she'd die anyway. At least her brat didn't die with her. And he would have too. You think after all this time somebody would have come looking if they wanted him." All her son said was *perhaps*. "You're going to fix this for me. I'm out of work, and I don't have any money because of you. Now someone has convinced *my* son that he needs to cut ties with me. And I want that sister too. I don't even care what you have to do to make that happen. Like I said, you owe me."

"We don't owe you crap, Melville. In fact, if I could, I'd make things harder on you. You're a bad man and a terrible role model for that young man, and I for one am glad that he's quit you. And you'll never get one of our dragons. Not so long as I have breath in my body. And speaking of which, you do not want me to mess with you and my breath, buddy. But as for all this bad luck you seem to be having? I believe that you did that all on your own." Elissa lifted her chin up when Melville drew back to hit her. "Do it. And you won't have to worry about where your next meal is coming from. I will tear you the fuck apart, and then bury you so deep that no one will ever find you."

He walked away, and Elissa turned to speak to her son. But Danburn was laughing with the oddest expression on his face. When she asked him what was wrong, it took him a few minutes to be able to answer her.

"You said *fuck*. Just like you used it every day." She crossed her arms over her chest and glared at him while patting her foot. It usually worked, but not today apparently. "Oh no you don't. You're not allowed to be mad at me when you're the bad guy in this. To think, my sainted mother said a bad word and the world didn't come crashing down on her head. I love it."

"I most certainly am not sainted. And if you breathe one word of this conversation to any of my new family, I will never speak to you again. So help me, Danburn—" He pulled her to him and kissed her on the forehead. There wasn't a better way for him to show his love for her than to give her a hug. "You must think I'm a hypocrite."

"No, I think that you're the most amazing woman that I've ever known, and you fight for justice whenever you need to. Even going so far as to curse and use the word right. I love you, Mom. More and more every day." She looked up at him. "Mom, how did I forget that you are so incredible?"

"You have a wife that outshines us all, and she's not afraid to curse when she needs to. Even when she doesn't need to, she can curse like a sailor." He agreed with her on that one. "I love you, son. And I'm so excited to be a grandmother to your daughter."

"Me too. A daughter to watch grow up into a fearsome dragon. And to play with her in the yard or take a long walk with her. I think I will be the happiest man alive once she is in our lives. To be honest, I didn't think I could be this happy. Having a child? Well, that sure does top the list of things I never thought would happen to me." She held him tightly and then backed away. "We should see what trouble our dear Sapphire is in."

"You think that she's in trouble?" Elissa just looked at him. "Yes, well, you could be right. But I've no doubt that she can get herself out of it just as easily. Besides, I think she and Denny can help young Mel much more than anyone can at this point. I think the young man already thinks of her as some kind of mother figure. Mel couldn't do any better with Denny as his father figure either. He raised himself three fine sons."

"That much is true." She thought of the sisters and what they were going to think once they were released. "She said that they're going to move into the houses if they wish. I hope they do. It'll give Dana and her so much more time to have fun."

"You mean sex?" She smacked him on the arm as they walked to the car. "I don't doubt that they'll be announcing they're having a baby soon too. They're as bad as Kendrick and I are about...having fun."

"Danburn, I swear there are times when I wish I had beaten you more." He pointed out that she never had beaten him. Not once in all these years. "Perhaps it's not too late to take up the habit. I'd need a large stick."

They were both laughing as they got into the car. She was going to love having all the children around. And she was already gathering up things about their grandpa that she could show them. They were going to know him as well as they did her.

~~~

Dana went to his office on the upper floors just as Sapphire came into the house. Christ, he loved that woman, and she only had to be close enough for him to touch to be in a better frame of mind too. When she came to him with open arms, he kissed her hungrily and picked her up from the floor so that she was wrapped around him.

"You do, and you'll never know what happened today." She giggled as he carried her up the stairs. "Oh Dana, how did I ever make it in this world without you? You're the sweetest, most romantic man I've ever known. Although, I've not known that many men."

"Nor will you from now on either. As for your day, I'm sure you did just fine. Did anything happen that caused death, bleeding, and/or someone who is going to have to be killed by me?" She told him not so much. "Good. I'm going to have you for my dinner, as Mrs. Crocket has gone home to fix dinner for her husband. I guess he had a wonderful day as well."

"He did. We all did. Mel knows about Melville not being his father. Melville has been told that he is no longer allowed to come near Mel. And not by me, but Mel. He really stood up for himself." He told her that was enough. "But there is so much more. Don't you want to hear about the clean up

123

we did today? Or the shipment of buckets we got in? They're beautiful."

"Buckets are not beautiful, even I know that, and no, I don't want to know about your clean up or anything else you did while not with me today." He laughed when he had trouble with the door. "Christ, you're a handful, aren't you?"

Pushing the door open with his foot, he threw her on the bed and watched her breasts as they bounced several times before he was naked. Magic made having quickie sex so much easier. But once he touched her, there was no need to hurry, he realized, and lifted her legs up to his shoulders.

"I love the way you taste when you're all wet. How your skin is all dewy with need." He kissed the inside of her leg, just below the knee. "The way that your toes curl up when you're aroused. And your nipples are tight against your shirt. You need to wear silk all the time, love, so I can see them when they're as hard as my cock seems to be all the time."

"You're taking too long. Talk less and take me faster. I thought that this was going to be a quickie." He told her that he'd changed his mind. "Well, then I'm going to tell you about— Yes, that's it. More."

He devoured the small nubbin, nibbled on her nether lips as he slid his fingers in and out of her. Just seconds, that was all it took for her to fill his mouth with her cream and to soak his hand. Dana loved how responsive her body was for him. The way that she screamed out her releases. There was just too much to list about things he loved about this woman—his woman.

"More, I need you, please, Dana." He blew over her clit, then licked the entire length of her. Each time he did that, tasting more and more of her, she would scream that it was

124

much too much, or that she needed more. Moving up her body, he made a feast of her navel. Suckled at her breasts. If he could have, he would have bitten her luscious ass. Taken her from behind while he was back there. Christ, he was hard as stone and almost in pain with it. "You better fill me or I'm coming again without you."

Slamming forward, he filled her with his cock. Sapphire held onto him so tightly, both his cock and his body, that he could barely move. Sliding over her, taking her throat to his mouth, he bit down just hard enough to make her come again, then he moved quickly in and out of her. He now needed to come. Needed to empty deep within her one more time. Christ, she was as hot as she was wet.

"Come for me, love. Milk my cock while I empty myself into you." Shaking her head, she told him she was done. "Nay, you are not. Come for me, Sapphire, and show me your lights."

He'd known that she would sparkle like her namesake when she came hard enough. He'd caught a glimpse of it just this morning when he'd taken her. And again in the shower today. But now he wanted to see it, watch her come with him as she showed him all that she was. When her wings spread out under her, he thought she was going to shift, but the wings were the light that he needed to see.

"Christ, you're beautiful." He took her hard, slamming his cock deep within her, so hard that he was sure she'd be sore in the morning. But when she screamed out that she loved him, that she would forever, his own climax raced over his body and seemed to erupt from his cock like it had been too full a bottle of soda and it released its build up. They came together, the two of them, and Dana felt his world simply

125

black out as he dropped over her.

When he woke she was still beneath him and he rolled to his back, leaving her lying there on the bed. Dana wasn't even sure that he could have lifted her up even should the house be on fire. Instead, when his knees were less shaky, he got up and pulled the blankets that had ended up on the floor over her. Dana made his way to use the bathroom and to wash his face.

He looked in the mirror at his sigil. Ferne was there, and he knew that she wasn't able to hear him when he didn't say her name first. Calling to her when he wrapped a towel around him, he asked her if she could find out about the man he'd seen in town earlier.

She sat on the counter now, her body much smaller than when he'd first spoken to her. Ferne told him it was because she didn't need to waste energy on enlarging herself when small would do just fine. It was all right with him too. Less scary being in the bathroom with her alone and semi naked.

"The man that crossed the street when you were at the bakery?" He said that was him. "I have looked, my lord. Other than having a gun and a knife on him, there is very little that I can find. The hotel has him as Smith. The car he has is a rental. Also under Smith. He has not asked for anyone that I can tell, but he does have a picture of the child and sister."

"Carmine." She said she'd not yet met her, but knew of her from his thoughts. "This man, can you see what's in his mind? I mean, is he here for Carmine?"

He wasn't sure how it worked, but when she left the counter to go to the window, he opened it for her and she took off. It occurred to him, too late he supposed, that she was going to a strange man's bedroom, and as it was well after

126

midnight, perhaps she would have sex with him. Not that he cared, but it was a strange thought. Dana went to check on Sapphire and took the sisters with him as he dressed for the conversation that he was going to have with them.

"Come to me, sisters three." They were suddenly in the room with him, and they sat down on the couch, a little shaken from the shift. "I have something I'd like to ask you. Sapphire is all right, but currently sleeping. But I have a plan to bring out the man who seeks you." He told them what he wanted to do.

"You have thought this through, have you not?" Opal had been a great deal nicer to him since she'd found out that he wasn't her mate. "I think that will work. But it will take a bit out of us. To switch around like that, one body to the next, we won't be able to help you should it turn nasty."

"I think we can handle him. What worries me is where he's getting his magic. I found out today that the woman he killed to take the baby was indeed having a diabetic issue, and had he stayed with her or even called someone, she'd be alive right now. Her husband, as you can imagine, is devastated, as well as her parents. They've been searching for the missing child since. The only reason that they're sure it was a boy is because of the DNA left behind."

Ferne came back just as he was explaining how things were going to work with the man. "He is alone in this. He has told no one that he is seeking to capture a dragon. And he is very upset with your mate, as well as Elissa, for keeping the dragons out of his reach." She introduced herself to the others, and they in turn took a bit of her so that she could help them too should they need it. Ferne looked at Dana when she had a seat. "The man you saw in town worked with the other man, Ramon, but he's not after the dragons, but the little girl. He has heard of her magic. The hotel where he is staying is paid up for the week by cash. There is plenty of money in his room, but it is tainted, with some kind of human drug. I think he stole the money. He has read the notes that he's found on Ramon's desk while he was cleaning it out. No one knows that he is here, nor do they have any idea that he's here for the little girl. Just a man on vacation, or so it looks like to them."

She smiled then and looked at him. "You did something to him." Ferne nodded then put her finger to her lush lips. "I don't want to know. I just.... Please, never give me details about how you get your information."

"I don't understand. I know what you are, but I…you have sex with men, correct?" Ferne explained to Opal what she did. "Ah. I wondered if a man's wet dream was indeed your kind. All this time, they blamed it on thoughts. It was you. Ha! I love it."

"I have been around for centuries, having men succumb to my wildest dreams. Making men do as I wished, when I wanted. But the last days here, with this new master, I am the happiest I have ever been. I have a purpose for the first time in my life." Dana thanked her. "Nay, my lord, it is I who thanks you." She stood up then. "I must leave. It is very taxing, and I should like to rest. Call to me when you need me."

She moved to him and was gone. He could feel her climbing her way to his back, and wondered briefly why she didn't just go there in the first place. She told him she must enter where a man thinks, then laughed at him when he felt his body heat in embarrassment.

The rest of the time was spent on the plan. It would work; they just had to make sure that at some point, Melville went beyond just harassing them to breaking the law. Once that happened, he could be brought in for questioning on other things like the death of the woman, because his DNA would then be in question. Sapphire joined them about the time they were sitting down to breakfast.

"I've got some news on the new greenhouse. There are several that have gone under in the last years and we can buy all their supplies, and this is a quote, so we can have it to sell it to the next person when we go under. Bastard." Em asked what sort of things they were doing now. Dana had forgotten how much they'd missed. "The new greenhouse, Dragon's Breath of Fresh Air, is a project that will help with the gardens. And will employ a lot of people. I mean, fifty of them when not busy, then during planting season, more for growing things. I have everything written down so that you'd not miss a thing."

After explaining that, Sapphire went to their room to get her notes. As she went over them—had it only been a few days?—the women were brought up to date on all the goings on with Mel and his non-father. Dana thought of his plan. He had a feeling that not only would his plan work, but it would make the man a little on the insane side as well. Not having a home or food would make him a little nutty too. Well, nuttier.

As the other women went to see their new homes and to start on the plan, Sapphire sat down with him. She looked so beautiful that, unable to help himself, he pulled her into his lap for a deep and wonderfully sexy kiss. Sapphire smiled at him when she lifted her head from his.

"I love you so very much." He told her that he loved her as well. "But you're keeping me from my work. I have to go out today, as do the others. And you must work on your faerie

129

home."

"That's it." He nearly dropped her on the floor when he stood up. "Faerie Home. That's the name of the piece. I couldn't get beyond calling it the log project. But I love Faerie Home." He wanted to go right down and work on it. He had so many ideas for it running through his head that he was nearly to the stairs when he came back and kissed Sapphire again. "You're the very best thing that has ever happened to me. I love you. Faerie Home. Perfect."

Chapter 8

Ruby walked along the sidewalk, continually getting distracted by the pretties in the shop windows. She so loved new clothes and the feel of silk on her body that she kept forgetting to keep an eye out for the man who was trying to hurt them.

Her job today was to be out and about dressed as her sister Em. The green did look good on her, and she loved her hair. When she'd made it all green as her sister did, she didn't much care for it and had streaked some red in it just for show. Now she was glad that she had. She looked fabulous. Then she saw the man coming from across the street.

She was supposed to talk to him, but she had a better plan in mind. Not that she'd use her plan because she didn't want to get hurt. As Wrinkle, her little puppy, barked, she knew that he'd seen him as well. Wrinkle was a large three headed jackal, and one that she loved a great deal. And while Wrinkle didn't care for the tiny pink bow in his hair, it was expected, so he tolerated it from her.

"Hello." She nodded to the man. Mr. Melville James wasn't one to mess with at the moment. "I was just looking for you. You and your sister, you've been hiding out from me."

"Have we? I wasn't aware that I even knew you. May I ask your name?" He told her. "Ah, then we have nothing to say to each other. And you're not looking for me, but for my sister, Em. I'm Ruby."

"But you're wearing green and— You said your name is Ruby? Then there are three of you?"

"No, just the one, me. What is it you think you want from me? Or from Em for that matter?" He told her he wanted the gems. "I have none now. I mean, once we hide them around the world, then we have none for a while. It's like draining a pot that's empty."

"I don't understand."

So she used the analogy that Rette's lovely wife had come up with. "Have you ever had the shits? Well, when you're over that, you're feeling pretty empty. Drained. That's what I am. I've shitted out all my gems and I won't have any more until later. Much later. Besides, what good would they do for you? You know that if you saturate the market with them, they'll be pretty much worthless. Not that they aren't that way now. No one uses real gems when the perfect man-made ones are so much better. Not to me, but to—"

"Shut up." She closed her mouth but smiled at him. "You talk a great deal, but don't say anything that I want to hear."

"That much is obvious." He glared at her but said nothing. "You're the person that stole Mel away from his mother. She was so ill that day, did you know that? Having a baby while being a diabetic is hard, but harder still when someone comes along and slits your throat. Did you enjoy that? Killing that poor woman?"

"Why is everyone so hung up on that? She was a druggie, not a diabetic. Don't you think I could tell the difference?" She asked him if he thought he could, because to her, he couldn't. "So you say. But I want you to come along with me. You'll see I'm not demanding but asking you nicely, and if you talk to Lord Danburn, you can tell him that."

"Let me get this straight. You want me to come along with you quietly and then you'll tie me up. You didn't say that but it's implied, wouldn't you say?" He looked confused again, but she didn't care at this point. "You're going to drain me as much as you can with my gems, sell them off to the highest bidder, then you'll start all over again when that is all gone. Oh, and I'm to tell Danburn, who I don't think likes you, that you asked me nicely to come with you. And apparently, you think that's enough."

"What is wrong with you? You jabber on and on, but you just aren't saying that much." He put out his elbow for her to take, like they were going on an outing or a date. "Come on then. We have work to do."

"No, you don't want to hear what I have to say, that's what it is. You're a moron." He told her there was no need for name calling. "You're an idiot too. I'm not going with you. I don't care how nicely you ask me."

"I just don't understand you people." She asked him what he didn't understand. "You want things to go nicely for you, but when a man is nice, you're all hot and mean. I need you to come along with me. Please. There now, I've been nice about it two times, and I think that's about the last time too."

"Well, good. I'd hate to have to keep repeating myself to

you. No, I'm not going with you. No, I'm not going to be your money maker. And hell no, I'm not going to be nice to you." She looked over the man's shoulder and saw Opal there. "You might want to try this crap on my sister."

When her sister smiled at Melville, she could see that it didn't mean that she was happy to see him. Instead, she looked as if she might just murder him where he stood. But when he smiled back, Opal took a step back from him. She didn't like people nearly as much as Ruby did.

"Are you going to be cooperative with me?" She told him more than likely not, but what did he want. "I'm going to have me a sign made for you people. It'll say, come with me, please, I want to get some gems from you for money. There now, does that explain what I want?"

Opal looked at her. "Is he for real?"

Ruby told her that he was. She realized that Opal was dressed all in red and it looked good on her. "You look beautiful. I think you should give red a chance. It really does bring out the opal color of your eyes. I wish I could have red eyes while out and about. I so love the way people shy away from me."

"They think you're a demon. And that's not good either. Remember that one time, oh about fifty years ago, when that maid threw holy water over you? He was screaming about possession and demons? I laughed so hard when you berated him for ruining your—"

"I'm standing right here and waiting." She'd actually forgotten about Melville. "Why don't you ladies come along with me and you can talk about anything you want. Having rubies and emeralds will be just the thing for me."

"I don't have emeralds. Neither does she." Ruby started

away as Opal did. He grabbed both their arms and started dragging them his way. "What the fuck are you doing?"

"I've been trying to find a way to use that word too. I love it. So mean sounding, and you can also use it in a good way. Like 'fuck me.' Do you think there are other words like that?" Ruby told Opal that she did think there were a lot of them that meant two things, depending how you said them. "Like the word love. Have you noticed how people say that all the time? 'Love ya.' I don't even know what that means. Ya. Is it a shortened version of 'you'? It's not even spelled the same. Is it an endearment? If so, why? There are—"

"Jesus H. Christ, don't you two ever shut the fuck up?" He looked at them both, and she could see all the niceties that he was showing were all gone now. "See, I used it too. Now, come with me or I'll have to get rough with you. And shut that fucking dog up before I have to shoot it too."

Putting her puppy down to the ground, she called his name. In seconds Wrinkle grew to his normal size, and heads were sprouted from his shoulders. Her puppy was now her jackal.

"Wrinkle, this man is going to rough us up. Do you have anything to say about that?" He spit fire at his feet, which had Melville jumping back from them. "Good boy. Now, why don't you chase this nasty man back to his place? But no hurting him. Unless he tries to hurt you. Then you can kill him."

When they were running down the road, she laughed. This was the most fun she'd had in ages. Not to mention how much fun she was having being able to talk to her sister without arguing. Wanting to continue on this vein, she asked Opal to lunch. As they went towards the little restaurant that served the most divine meal called hot dogs, she told Opal that they needed to go out more.

"I agree. It's been too long since we've been able to have fun." They had sat on the deck last night and watched the dragons flying through the sky. It had been so long since any of them had seen such a sight.

Dana was a true gem diamond. His was smaller than the others, but still very large. His wings glistened, even in the moonlight, and stars seemed to reflect back at them when he dove around the sky. And when he was in that form, not only were his eyes an icy blue as the coldest ice, but he was also scarier. His dragon would only need to blow his fiery diamonds over someone before he could break them into a million colorful diamonds so that they'd never be found. And the really scariest part was, you would not necessarily die. Yes, you would be broken into tiny shards, but that didn't kill you if you were an immortal.

Opal was very lucky that he'd not hit her the day that he'd sprayed her with his breath. She was one of the creatures that would live through eternity as pieces of diamonds. Perhaps even as someone's bauble.

~~~

The home was coming along nicely. He'd been working on it for several hours now, and the faeries were forming just the way he'd thought they would in his mind. And being able to cut the gems into thin slices was making it so that the wings that he had envisioned were perfect as well. Wrapping pewter around one of the slices of opal, he looked up when someone cleared their throat. Smiling at Carmine, he asked her what she thought of his art.

"It's very beautiful. Can I touch it?" He told her to be

gentle, and when she put her finger to one of the many wings that he'd yet to attach to the small people, she smiled at him. "They're warm, aren't they?"

"They are. I asked Sapphire about it, and she said it was because I was putting my heart into each piece. I'm having a good time with this. By the way, how did the tea go? I forgot to ask Hanson about it." She grinned. "That good, huh? I know that Sebastian was excited to be able to go with you."

"He was so charming, my teacher called him. And when he sat at my feet, no one made fun of me or anything. One of them asked me why I'd brought him instead of my mom, and before he could say anything else, Sebastian told him to sit down and to be quiet because he was being rude. I think him talking freaked them out a little." Dana said it had him the first time he'd heard Sebastian speak. "Yes, his voice is so deep."

"So, no one bothered you anymore after that?" She smiled and then giggled. He loved seeing her so happy. "I'm happy for you. I know that you were upset a little about what was going on."

"Grandma Elissa told me that I should just let it be like the waterfall in the back of their castle. Just let it roll off, because I'm more than they'll ever be. But I was strong enough not to abuse my power when they hurt my feelings." She giggled again. "She said she would have turned into her dragon and took them all out. But I did much better than she had. She'd not do that, would she?"

"I don't know, to be honest. When I was very young, I lost both my parents. They'd been cocky, I know that now. They tempted fate every time they showed themselves to humans. And even leaving behind a part of them, a few scales now and then, it wasn't enough. So one night, whilst I slept in the castle with the servants, my parents decided to go for a long walk as humans. The men who attacked them had wanted them to shift after they were dead, thinking that was the way it worked since they were humans when they died. I guess they thought it would be a big deal for them, and a profitable one, for them to kill the dragons." She told him she was sorry. "So am I. But when Elissa heard about their deaths, she came to get me and to take me back to their home to grow up. I had a grandmother, but she didn't want me. Anyway, the very first night I was at her home, the very first night, Elissa went back to the town and burned the men's houses down, right to the ground. There was no saving them from the heat of one so powerful as she is."

"Wow. She really did it." He nodded at her, watching her face for her to be upset with the woman. "I loved her before, Uncle Dana, but knowing that she would do something like that for someone that she loves, I love her even more."

"Good. I was afraid you'd be scared of her." Carmine told him never would she be afraid of her grandma. "Elissa is the best there is and loves with all her heart. You remember that."

"I will, I promise." She wandered around the room and he watched her as he worked. There was more on her mind, and he decided that he'd just let her come to him about it. He wanted to slay.... Well, slay dragons for her, but she'd not allow him to do that. Not when someone as powerful as her could take care of herself. "The men are coming soon. But that'll be all of them if they don't find me."

"Do you think they will?" She said that they would. "Then what can we do to figure this out so that no one comes here again for you?"

She shrugged, then told him what she thought. "I could kill them and the people that they work for. I don't think that'll stop them. People will want to know what happened to them." He said that was for sure. "I don't want to go to the lab. I hoped that the last guy would be all there was."

"Yes, honey, but the motion was set before you came here. And I bet that if your mom was here now, she'd tell you that she's more than sorry that this is happening to you and your sister." She nodded. "If it makes you feel any better, I can tell you about the time that I was captured."

"What happened? Was there blood and guts?" He looked at her, shocked. "I'm joking. I love saying stuff like that to you guys; you're so funny when you think I'm serious."

"All right then, that's enough frightening stuff for one day." She begged him to tell her about being captured. "This was a very long time ago, you understand, and it was before there were computers or even phones in homes. A few houses had them—I did, but not everyone was as rich as I was. Understand?"

"Yes. Dragons can make pretty gems out of tears, and you're one of the ones that makes diamonds." He said that was right, but few people knew that, Even back then. "I won't tell anyone."

"I know that, honey. So anyway, I was a very wealthy man living in my castle." She asked him if he still had it. "Yes, it's in Ireland. I'll have to take you there someday. But we all have them. Danburn is the only one that I know that actually lives in his. But I digress. I was a wealthy man taking a moonlit stroll with a lovely lady. It was surprising to me that she was in on it. I guess her demur actions belied the fact that she was a money grubbing who—woman that had very few morals."

139

"She was a whore. I know the word, Uncle Dana." He was embarrassed, and nearly cut his hand off with the glass cutter when she continued speaking. "I guess women had to do what they could to make ends meet. Even if they had to sleep around to do it."

"Yes, well...I'm not ready for you to know about sex." She laughed at him. "Laugh if you will, but to me you will always be too young and too our little girl to be having sex. Even after you're married, you can't be having sex."

"Like that's going to work." He could see a little more of Hanson and Quinn in this kid all the time. "But you were taking a stroll in the moonlight."

"I was, with Bea. As we were turning the corner to head back to my home, these men, ruffians we called them back then, came out of nowhere and attacked. I should have noticed sooner that she wasn't touched by them, but they hit me with a large club." She was staring at him with rapt attention. "I was down and out for a few minutes, enough time for them to pick my pockets clean and to take my coin bag with diamonds in it. When I woke, I was very quiet and saw Bea counting out the money and diamonds for them. One for them, and two for her, she was telling them."

"You saw her working with them? What a terrible person. I hope you got her in the end." He did, but he'd not tell her that part. He thought her bloodthirsty enough. "What happened next?"

"She knew what I was. I don't know how she figured it out, but since she knew what I was, she had me chained up. The iron was cutting into my legs so I shifted a little. Having the diamonds on my skin is why I was able to get away from them." He put the little faerie in the small opening on the log he was working on. "Once I was free, they scattered to the four winds and I gave chase as my dragon. One of the biggest mistakes I've ever made. They saw me; the entire town saw me as a dragon, and I was no longer safe to be there."

"How did they know it was you?" Dana told her that Bea had screamed out his name, just before she died. "You killed her, didn't you? You had to do it, Uncle Dana. Like the people coming after me, if you don't, then they think that they've won. I don't want that any more than you did to become their captive."

"No, I don't want that. But killing someone is very hard on your heart. Especially as young as yours is." She nodded. "It's true what they say about killing someone and their blood stains your hands forever. I have plenty of stains on my hands."

She took his hand in hers and looked it over. He was ready to tell her that it was an old saying when she looked him in the eyes. He saw her magic then. Like stars on the dark night, the magic twinkled in her eyes just like that. A twinkle. But a deadly one, he was sure.

"What do you see when you look at your hands?" He said that's not what he meant. "I know that. You were proving a point. So am I. What do you see when you look at your hands? Tell me."

"Years of scars from doing what I could to survive. All of them, all my scars, they have a story to tell as well. How I did it. Who was with me when it happened." She asked him if he wanted to know what she saw. "I do, very much so."

"I see my Uncle Dana. A man who survived all these scars and the ones on your body that are larger and deeper in your flesh. I see hands of a man that has been helpful too. To a little

141

girl that asks too many questions when he only wants to work. But you want to know what I see that is the most important of all?" He nodded. "I see your hands. I see them because you killed to still be here. You worked hard so as not to be a lazy man. I see all of you because you're the nicest person I know, and you'd never harm anyone without needing to so that you could survive, to be here with me right now."

He hugged her to him, tightly, and wondered where the child had gotten to be so good at making people feel good about themselves. Kissing her on the top of her head, he pulled her back slightly and told her that he loved her. When she kissed him on the cheek, he felt as if he could take on the world with her beside him and come out not just on top, but as ruler as well.

They talked about his project, and she wanted to figure out the price for him. It was fun watching her come up with a reasonable pay per hour for his work. To him it wasn't work, but something he did to relax himself, to feel good about something that he was working on.

"How much do you charge for my heart to be in each piece?" She said that was what made the piece so special, it was him in a nutshell. "Well, I don't think anyone would care how much I hate to see each piece I do depart from my studio."

"I bet they would. I would. But then, I can see your heart on each piece you have in here. You give a little of yourself to everything you do." He nodded as he shaved the sapphire for the wings of the next tiny faerie. "She's going to love this, isn't she? Aunt Sapphire. She's going to love this piece so much. As much as I do."

"I hope someone likes it. It's enough, I hope, to pay off

this building and buy more supplies." He had explained to her that he didn't dip into his diamonds unless he really had to. Which thankfully, so far, he'd not had to. As the day wore on, they were having so much fun, he realized that they'd not had lunch and it was coming up on dinner, and he'd not heard from Sapphire all day. Reaching out to her, he realized that she was unconscious and that alarmed him more than anything. His mind went into overdrive thinking of all the things that could have happened to her.

Chapter 9

The pallets were pulled off her, but she still felt as if she was being weighted down. She knew that she was spreading herself very thin, but there was so much to do now that she had everyone doing something for her. Dragon's Breath was going to open in a few days, and she thought things could have been better, but the paper had come out to interview them and had run that they'd be opening an entire month before they'd planned. Well, things happened, and they had worked so hard to get this far.

"Are you all right?" Dana looked frantic and she asked him what he was doing there. "I felt that you'd been hurt, and I came as fast as I could."

Getting out of the mess of pallets, she dusted herself off and told him she was fine. "Better than fine, I'm fantastic." He touched his fingers to her forehead and they came away bloodied. "It's a little blood. I'll heal before you know it. Seriously, you have to stop pampering me so much."

"I love pampering you, and I don't think that asking you

not to use a chair to see what's on the top shelf of our cabinets is pampering you. I'm trying to protect you." She said it was the same thing. "No, it's not. Never mind. What happened here that made you perfectly safe when a wall of pallets fell atop you?"

"I don't care for your tone." Dana told her that he didn't care for her bleeding either, but they had to live with them both. "All right. I might have thought things through just a little more before I climbed up on the ladder to throw one of the pallets on top of the stack. It wasn't really a stack so much as a mountain of pallets that we're going to burn."

"People pay good money for them—don't burn them just yet. Why were you thinking that the mountain of pallets needed to be just one more taller? You have a death wish, is that it?"

"Yes, that's it. I wish to be crushed to death by smelly old pallets that needed to be gotten rid of years ago. People really do buy them? How much do you think I could get for all of these?" He told her he didn't know. "I'll look it up."

"Maybe they'd be worth more if they have a bit of your brain matter on them. Maybe you can try it again, but this time actually bust your head open. I'll even take pictures." She had to walk away or kill him. "Oh, I know, you could send it into that show that does funny videos all the time. I'm sure you'd take first place."

"I don't like you." He grinned at her. "Don't be charming either. You've been making fun of me since you arrived. I don't care for it."

"Then please be careful. I was happily working on my piece when I realized that we'd not eaten lunch." Sapphire asked him who he'd been with. Not jealous, just curious.

"Carmine. She was talking to me about her day at the school, which went well, and I was telling her about my life as a young dragon. Are you really all right?"

"I am, I promise." He nodded and kissed her. "We're about ready. Some of the inventory is going to be a little late to get on the shelves, but the pack said that they'd make sure that it was ready when we closed that night if it gets here after we open."

"It looks really good. I love the big half barrels you have out front. Were they salvaged from one of the other greenhouses?" She told him where she'd gotten them. "I bet there is a lot of crap in that old barn back there. And the shed that is out to the left of the greenhouses. You have them going up well too."

"We aren't going to be able to plant anything this year to have it in time for summer, but we did order in some things we think will sell. And if any of the herbs that I ordered don't sell, Denny said that we should plant them along the sidewalks so that when people stepped off them, they'd have a nice treat. I know I've been having fun in our garden."

"Yes, we have tomatoes, I guess. A little early, but the cook said that she helped it along a little. Do you supposed if you were to plant something for this year, the faeries could help you out as well?" She said she didn't want to ask, not this year. "Probably a good thing. Also, you should know that there are some things in Elissa and Danburn's barn. Old stuff that occasionally she goes through and throws things out. You might want to have a look for displays. I know that there is a Formica table in there with six chairs that used to be in the maid's house before Elissa had it updated."

"I could use that. Do you think she'd care if we sold it

147

too? If someone wanted to buy it?" He told her that she'd more than likely be glad to get rid of it. "We're only using the money that we said we'd start with. I could redo this entire thing and have it up to date in no time. But I want to do this on my own. So if she won't mind selling me the table and chairs, I'll try my best to make a profit on it."

"Good for you." He asked her what else was going on. "I've made Mel the assistant manager. He and Denny are getting along well, and I think he might be bringing him out of his shell. Also, he has some great ideas for here too. Just the other morning, he suggested that we have a cash only register. We only got one credit card machine in so far."

"I don't have to tell you what would happen if his father showed up. You heard what happened to him and your sisters." She laughed and told him she wished that she was there. "Yeah, me too. How about this—we have dinner, you and I, then we head over to Danburn's to see about the barn. I can ask the pack to help clean it up, and everyone is happy. How many people you have working here right now?"

"Fourteen. It's been really nice having the extra hands here. And since they're mostly non-humans, it's easier on the humans that might not have the strength of their backs like they used to. Most of the people working here are about Denny's age." He nodded as he noticed that a group of them were starting to put a display together with Mel's help. "He works well with everyone, but he's not a pushover. Denny was coaching him at first, then it all seemed to click. And they all know that he has a disability as well, and we're working around that."

"He needed someone like you in his life a long time ago. Oh, and Kendrick found out who his grandparents and father are. They want to meet him. Roger, his father, has remarried and has three kids of his own now. And the grandparents are just happy to have closure as to what happened to him. They said that they had worried that he'd fallen into the wrong hands. I did tell them about Melville, though not his name. But they know we're aware of someone here that played a part in her death."

"I'll be glad when this is over. Not that I think it will turn out well for Mel, not with Melville making noises all over the place that Mel and I are having an affair." He asked her what she said. "Oh, don't worry about it. I have it covered. Danburn hates the little shit, and he's going to go and see him in the morning. Bright and early. He's in for a rude awakening if he thinks he's going to ask for one of the dragons. I had no idea that Danburn had never checked to see if the man was what he said he was. All this time, he's taken his word for it because he smelled like strong magic. Also, he is using up the last of his black magic. He'll either have to find more or it'll all come rushing back at him at some point. His age, the aches and pains he might have suffered. And if he's older than a man should be, say over a hundred and fifty, like we think that he is, he'll shrivel up and die without the police taking him in for questioning."

"Speaking of which, they're going to talk to him in the morning. I wonder if that's what Danburn is waiting for." She said she didn't know, but had to get back to work. "No more pallet stacking. And I bet you could get at least a couple of bucks a piece for them. But to be sure, put ten. If they don't sell, then lower the price. It's easier to lower than it is to make them higher at this point."

When he left her, she made sure that she had enough

people to stack the pallets five high. A sign was made for them, but someone that was in the back when she was getting the pallets repaired after their tumble told her to put twenty bucks on them and she'd still sell them all. While she was trying to figure out if she was going to be the laughing stock of the town for the price, a semi pulled into the lot. She'd not expected anything for at least another week.

"You the owner of this place?" She told the driver that she was. "I have a load here that I can't take back. I'm back hauling another trailer. My company told me that I was to get rid of it as best I could. The other greenhouse went under and no one bothered to tell us about it. Mark said I could sell it to you for fifty cents on the dollar."

"How do I know this isn't a scam?" He handed her his cell phone and the bill of lading. After making a call to Rette, she called the man on the invoice. "I'm the owner of Dragon's Breath, Sapphire Blankenship, and I have your driver here."

"Yes, yes, I know. He just called me to tell me that you're just opening up. Good for you. I'm the owner of Magical Beans. I know, it's a silly name, but that's what my daughter called it, and we've had it for several years now. The truck on your lot is worth a great deal of money. Most of it is plants, but there is inventory as well, a great deal of it. The order was for just over a hundred thousand dollars. If you can take it, I'll sell it to you for fifty cents on the dollar. All of it."

"I don't know, Mr. Mark. I'm new to this sort of thing." He told her that he'd sell it to her for twenty cents on the dollar. "Hang on a minute."

She told Rette what the name of the place was called that she was talking to, as well as the name of the man. He pulled out his cell and made what she thought was four calls. As soon as he came back to her, Rette told her to offer him fifteen cents on the dollar, and tell him that Danburn would pay for the shipping costs.

"Mr. Mark, I'm to offer you fifteen cents on the dollar, and Danburn English said that he'd pay the shipping." The man laughed and laughed a long time. "You know each other, I take it."

"Yes, we're good friends, he and I. I'll tell you what, Mrs. Blankenship, you order from me for the next six — no, make it for the next year, and I'll give you that entire load minus the cost of the driver. He'll need per mile on the load to you."

"To me. You mean from the other place that he was taking this to, or to me? That's what you said, by the way." He laughed again and told her from the first greenhouse to her. "Deal. And what do I do with this trailer? The man who drove it said that he has a back haul to take back."

"He does, for me. You have to keep it on your lot for a week and I'll have someone come back for it. Is that agreeable to you?" She asked him if he was honest, and Rette nodded just as the man said he was. "You can ask Danburn, but I'm pretty sure that he'll lie to you to make me look bad. Yes, I'm as honest as he is. On this, I give you my solemn oath."

The driver was nice enough to drive it to the back where the barn was. After he pulled it through the drive through like opening, he unhooked and left them standing there. She didn't have the first clue what she was going to do with a truck load of merchandise that she didn't order.

"All right now, this is what we're going to do. Make piles of whatever we have." Denny winked at her as he continued talking to the entire staff. "For now, we'll empty this sucker. After that we'll have more time to put it in the store front. I'm

151

to understand that there are some plants on here? Well, those will be dealt with by the planting crew. You know who you are?"

Almost as soon as they realized they didn't have nearly enough people for this sort of undertaking, a group of men and women showed up, via Danburn. He said that they were being paid by him, and that she was to work them until she was satisfied that they were done. It was the best five and a half hours she'd ever spent doing a dirty job like emptying a trailer.

~~~

Melville was just sneaking out of the apartment when he saw the police, as well as Danburn, coming down the hall. Before he could get back into his room and lock the door, they were on him and had him to the floor. No cuffs, which confused him, but he was helped up and told not to run.

"You come to tell me which woman I can have for my very own?" He looked at the men that were with him. "Did you know that he's a dragon? That he has more women at his house that are dragons too? They cry out gems."

"Mister, I don't care if he poops out mushrooms that grow into houses, you just stand there and listen up. These men have stuff to say to you." The mayor came running down the hall with a dirty pair of jeans on, as well as something on his face. He said he was sorry for being late. "Mayor, you're helping out with the truck too?"

"I am. I have to say, it's a lot more hard work than I thought it would be, but we're getting it done. Now, what is going on here?" Danburn told Rette what had happened yesterday when he'd harassed the women that were his guests for the moment. "I'm to understand that they've decided to stay, these women. Good for them. It's always nice to have newcomers come to town."

"Rette, you have dirt on your forehead, and if you wipe at it again with that dirty handkerchief, I'm going to take it from you." They laughed and Danburn continued. "Yes, they're going to stay. And in addition to the harassment charges I'd like to have brought against him, there is the matter of the young woman, Elizabeth Tucker. She was murdered, and her child was taken by Mr. James here."

"I did no such thing. My God, how many times are we going to go over this? I didn't do anything but take the baby when it was obvious that she was going to die."

Rette asked if she'd died by Mr. James's hand or something else.

"His. She was having a diabetic seizure, and had she gotten help when she needed it, she would have lived to see her child being born. Also, she left behind a husband and her parents, all of whom have been grieving for not just her death, but also the unknown whereabouts of her infant son."

"She was a drug addict, not diabetic—whatever. I demand that you stop bringing that up." Danburn finished his story with him slicing open her throat and then her belly to take the child. "No, that's not the way it happened at all. She was doped up and she.... Christ. That's it, she gave me the child for money."

"So, you're saying that you gave her money for her unborn child, and took it while she was still alive?" He nodded, then shook his head at Rette. "Which is it? You killed her after paying her for the baby? Or you paid for the baby then killed her?"

"I didn't do anything that she wasn't going to do in the

153

first place." He asked how a person was to slit their throat. "No, not that. It was necessary to take her life, in order for me to take the child without her screaming her fool head off. But she was going to die anyway. So you should be telling me what a good job I did rather than coming here and questioning me like I'm some sort of monster."

"You are. And since you've just admitted to killing the woman, I will sign the arrest warrant. You should have asked for an attorney, Mr. James. But since I've been here with the others, you never once said a word. And since you weren't arrested until after the confession, there is squat you can do about it now."

They'd tricked him. Just like on them shows he watched all the time, they'd tricked him into this. Now he was not only being read his rights, but he was also cuffed. He didn't want to go to jail, nor prison. He just wanted to get himself a dragon and live happily ever after.

"Danburn, how about you give me one of them women for about an hour? I can get me some bail money and get out of your town. You won't ever have to see me again." Danburn told him he was already getting that. "I don't want to go to jail, and you have a means to help me out with this. Just get the girls and make me some of their gems, then I'll go away. I'd like to take Mel—he's been very resourceful over the years, but he's mad at me right now. Maybe you could see your way in making that right for me too. It's the least you can do."

"No, you got that all wrong. The least I can do is turn my back on you and walk away. But I've made a promise and I aim to keep it." He asked what sort of promise. "Mr. Tucker, husband to the late Elizabeth Tucker, and her parents are here. They want to see the monster, their words this time, who took their first grandchild and then murdered their little girl."

"No, I'm not going to go see them. First of all, I have things to do today. As soon as you help me with my bail money by giving me that girl, I'm going to leave town. Remember me promising you that, Danburn?"

"We're not friends. Don't call me by my given name again." Melville couldn't understand what the big deal was. They were going to be partners in this thing; he'd give him some of the gems and Danburn would make some cash. Not that he needed it. From what he'd seen, Danburn— "You're going to jail, where they're waiting for you."

He wasn't going to jail, damn it. Melville wanted things to just once go his way. And when he was put into the cruiser to drive the less than hundred yards to the jail, not a single thought went through his head on how to get out of this situation.

As soon as he was let out of the cruiser, he saw Mel standing there. "Where the hell did you get that kind of money? And why are you wearing a suit? Somebody die?" He said his mother did. "Besides that; and it's not like you even knew her. For all you know I could be the one telling the truth and these men are lying to you."

"They're not. I'm here to meet my dad and my grandparents. I'm twenty-five years old, and I didn't know anything different than what you said to me. Now I have a whole family that, thankfully, doesn't include you." Mel looked him up and down before sneering at him. "You killed any chance I had in having a normal life. One where you didn't lie to me every day."

They entered the building that housed the cells that he

was being led to, but also the lost and found, he'd figured out, and a plethora of other small-town things. He was walked by a couple that looked like they were old enough to be Mel's grandparents, and another man that looked very wealthy. Melville thought that before this was finished, he'd see about getting a reward for bringing their little boy into the world and away from the druggie. He was going to come out smelling like a fucking rose before this was done.

The woman stopped his progression to the cell. "You the one that took my grandson?" He said that he was the one that saved him. Then she spit on his face. "You deserve whatever hell they can put you in, you murdering son of a bitch. You killed my daughter."

"No. Like I keep telling these guys here, she was full of drugs. I could smell them on her. And she was high as a kite when I took the baby. What was I supposed to do? Just leave it there for the other heathens? I saved his life, and that is what you should be thanking me for." She spit on him again. "Listen lady, I can understand why you're upset, but there isn't any reason for you to keep doing that."

"They found no drugs in her system when they did the autopsy. Not only that, but the cut that you slit across her throat, you mother fucker, didn't kill her until she bled out. You took her child from her while she was still alive. Then you just walked away. Had you checked her medical bracelet and given us a call about any of the things that happened that day, not only would I have my grandson, as we should have, but my daughter as well. You took them both from us."

"No drugs?" That wasn't right. There had to be drugs in her system. He'd seen her when she was begging him for a fix. Now that he thought on it, even after all these years, she did try to tell him that she needed a hit, not a fix. To him it had been the same thing, but perhaps she'd been telling him that she needed a shot or something. "Well, I'll admit to making a mistake on that one, but how was I supposed to know? I knew nothing about her sickness."

"You would have if you had read her medical record." He asked when he was supposed to do that. "The facts were on the bracelet that you stole. I'm assuming that it was you that took it. Right?" He had, but said nothing to the man now. "You monster."

"Now look here. I did bring the baby into the world. I did raise him to be mine. I did that, but you got no reason to be calling me a monster. I'm a person, just like you are, who made a mistake about something. You can't be blaming me for that, making a mistake. Nor can you go about calling me a monster. I'm just a man."

"You killed her." He looked at Mel and rolled his eyes. The dummy was going to speak now? Just what he needed. "You murdered her as surely as you're going to jail for what you did to me."

"Oh my, you look just like I did when I met your mother." The man, he had no idea what his name was other than Tucker, hugged Mel to him like he was his long-lost son. He supposed he was, really, but that wasn't any call for him to treat him the way he was. Mel had never hugged him. Not that he'd allow that. He didn't really care for him, not really.

"He's a dummy. Can't read nor write." The grandma asked if he was dyslexic just like his mom was. "Yeah, that's what they called it, but he can't read. It's why he's lost so many jobs and such. You should have seen his grade cards before the state put him in the special classes."

"Your mom had to be helped that way as well. They didn't know as much then as they do now about dyslexia. We'll get you some help and you'll be right as rain."

Mel hugged the elderly couple and Melville wanted to puke. But he was taken to his cell and was actually glad for it—the less he saw of them all fawning over each other, the better he liked it.

Chapter 10

Mel was at work the next morning after meeting his grandparents and dad. He wasn't sure what to call them, nor what to do with them. He'd given them a hug, just to see his — whatever Melville was to him — just to see him getting jealous. But now he was at a loss.

"You think you'll go and live with them?" Mel told Denny he didn't think so. "Did they at least ask you to come see them?"

"Yes. But I don't know. I told them that I'm trying my best to get my life together, and I love it here." He said he did too, that Sapphire was good to work for. "She gave me an advance on my next check for that new suit. She said that I have to make a good first impression — you don't get a second chance at that. This keeps up and I won't have a next check."

He knew how much he was making an hour, but he didn't have any idea how that would compute into his checks. Numbers were worse than letters in getting them all messed up. He supposed it was all right. Now not only did he have a

159

roof over his head and a place that he could call his own, but he had a car. It was old and sometimes had to be sweet talked to in order for it to start. It had been Kendrick's before she married Danburn. It had surprised him to find out that she'd been as broke as him when she'd married the king of dragons.

"You get them plants in the dirt over there and then we'll call it a day. I'm beat. And Sapphire told us to get to bed early, because of tomorrow being the grand opening and all." He was supposed to wear his dress shirt not his tee tomorrow, so that people would know that he was important. "I'm going to be working over here on the last of the trees. You holler if you need me."

He loved working with Denny. He was kind, and his wife had been just as nice as anyone he'd ever met. Every day that Denny and he worked together, he'd have a nice lunch from Mrs. Denny. That's what he called her, Mrs. Denny, and she got the biggest kick out of that. But tomorrow was going to be a big day, and he didn't want to mess it up. He thought he'd do much better knowing that his dad was put in jail.

Melville had killed his mom. How he'd done it, Mel wasn't sure. He'd heard two different stories. One, he'd shot her up full of drugs and taken him. The other, he'd cut him from her belly after cutting her throat. He believed that Melville could have done either one, but he believed the second one more than the first. It was like him to kill someone over anything.

Melville had been good to him, he supposed. He'd only cuffed him a couple of times in all their time together. Once he'd lost his temper with him and had put him in the hospital for a week when he'd gotten in trouble over his learning at school. Melville had wanted him to believe that it had been all his fault, but he knew better. He was a mean drunk, and a mean sober man too.

After getting the flowers in the barrel the way he liked them, he went to help out Denny. The man was a wonder at organizing things, and he just put things where he wanted them. It was his way to do things, and since he'd never messed with his way of doing things, they got along just fine. After that, they headed to their homes.

He got the car to start on the first try. As he was driving home, careful of each stop sign and the town's single light, he thought about his life up until meeting Sapphire. She looked like she was about his age, maybe just a little older, but he knew her to be well older than even his grandma. She aged well, she'd told him when he'd asked her. Like that was a reason she was so beautiful. But instead of acting like his sister or something, she treated him more like she was his momma and he her son. It was a good feeling knowing that if he messed up, she'd protect him first, then tell him what a screw up he was later. Not that she did things that way, but that was what he felt like. She was his teacher, mom, and protector all rolled up in a pretty woman that loved him. And he loved her too.

He'd not said that to her. And he never would, he thought. She was good to him, and he didn't want to mess that up with emotions. Emotions, he knew, could get you into deep shit. Or so that's what Melville had told him. So far, the man had been a wealth of misinformed information, he was figuring out. Bullshit, that's what he knew that Sapphire would call it.

The knock at his door startled him. When he went to look see who it might be, he backed from the door at the woman standing there. Why would his grandma be coming here in the middle of the evening? Opening the door, he didn't invite her in, but it seemed moot since she came right on in anyway. Then his dad came in.

"I wanted to try and convince you to come and live with us. It'll be so nice having you there." He said that he didn't know just yet what he was going to do. "Yes, you do. You just don't want to tell me. You want to surprise me. Ask anyone I know, I hate them. Surprises, I mean."

"I don't know anyone you know." That took her back, he could see it on her face. "I'm not sure that I'd fit in with you all. I like things here, and since Melville is in jail, I think I'll be just fine. I'm glad that we've found each other, but—"

"You just don't understand. It's been twenty-five years, and I want my grandson to come home with me." He glanced at his dad, who never said a word unless he was asked something directly. And he never spoke to Grandma. "Roger, tell him that I need for him to come home with me. I need to have him there because of my daughter."

"You should listen to your grandmother, Mel. Did you know that we were going to name you William? It would have been Will too, not Bill." Grandma told him to shut up. Then she seemed to remember herself or something and asked him to please not babble. "Anyway, you should listen to her. It's easier."

The last was said very low. Like he knew she was hard of hearing and didn't want her to know it. Looking at her, at the woman that had given birth to his mom, he realized two things; she was a bully, and she wasn't nice to anyone. Not really.

"I want to stay here. It's my home and I have friends here." She started to cry, and he looked at his dad again, who just barely shook his head. This was the strangest conversation that he'd ever had. "I think I'd like for you both to go on home. I have a big day tomorrow, and I don't want to mess it up by being tired."

"You don't have to work. I have money." Not *we*, but I. He'd noticed that too about her. She was very possessive. "Come on now. You don't want to live like this when you could have everything you ever dreamed of. Now, let's get you packed up. Roger, see if he has anything nice to wear home. And see — "

"I've decided that I want to stay here." But she ordered Roger around like he was her maid or something. "Did you hear me? I don't want to go with you. I want to stay here. I have a job, and this is my home."

"You'll see. Once you get to my house, you'll see all that you've been missing." He said he couldn't miss what he didn't know. "You're being obtuse right now, and I don't care for it, Elizabeth."

The room seemed to just pause in that moment, like the house knew what she said but it was waiting for someone to confirm it. When Roger stopped moving toward his bedroom and stood next to him, he thought for sure they were going to just take him away and not care a fig for his opinion.

"You've done this, and he said no." Dad's voice had gone hard then. Before it was all buttery, like a stick of it that had been out in the sun too long. "You and I should go. He's made himself perfectly clear that he wants to stay here."

"But he's my only connection to my daughter." Mel told her that he wasn't the daughter but a full-grown man. "And that man, that monster, took her from me. I want you to come home with me, damn it. I have a lot of years to make up for."

"I'm not a dog, lady, that you can take home and paper

163

train. I'm a man who has a job, a house, and all the stuff that I love. The person that I work for, Sapphire? She's been the best for me. Giving me a chance when nobody else would. I didn't need you in my life before, and if you're going to try and bully me around, I've already had that. And so you know, I don't need a keeper. I think you should go home now."

Mel went to the door, his back feeling like it was stronger than he'd ever had it feel. Even his mind was clear on what he was doing. He was standing up for himself, something that he'd not had a lot of practice in for his entire life. When he opened the door, he stood there while she cried. He wanted to tell her that tears didn't bother him. But the truth was, they cut him to the quick.

"I just don't know what to do." She sat down on his couch, but he didn't move. "She was taken from me, and we'd had a fight. I don't remember what it was about."

"Yes, you do. You fought with her about me." Dad sat down on the couch too, and he thought about just going to bed but wanted to hear this. "You have never liked me, Beth. Never even after it was figured out that I didn't kill my wife. You still blamed me."

"You should have taken better care that she didn't get killed." Dad stood up then and came to stand in front of him. "Roger, please, I'm sorry. I shouldn't have said that."

"I'm glad you did." Dad looked at him. "You're just what I had hoped for in a son. A good man, a better man than I am. You keep right on standing up for what you want and what you believe in. And if you'd not mind, I'd like for you to meet your half-sisters and brother."

"I'd like that too. I've been an only child for all my life." They laughed. "You know where I live, you come on back and see me anytime. But call first. I'm going to be making some money now, and I might be working."

Hugging his dad felt different this time. It was meaningful. He hugged him a second time when he started to release him. And when they parted, he noticed that he was crying like he was. After shaking hands, he left him there. His dad wasn't coming back to make him go with his grandma and would probably leave town as soon as he got his things. That's the way it should be, he thought.

"Grandma, I want you to go home." She started crying again. "Won't work on me. I told you, I don't know you all that well, but I have my own life, and tears from you aren't going to make me change my mind."

"I just wanted to be a part of your life." He told her no she didn't. "Yes, I did, Mel. I really wanted to make you happy."

"You wanted to run my life, and we both know it. You would have had me all dressed up in a suit every day, meeting people that you know and doing what you wanted. I don't want that, you do. You want to be a part of me, then you have to realize I have my own thoughts and ways of doing things." She nodded. "Your head is saying yes, but I can see that you're not going to give up. I'm not going back with you. I love what I have here. You have to get on with your life, Grandma, or you'll be a sour old woman that nobody wants to be around."

"When she left that morning, I was so mad at her. She and Roger were going to move to California for a year. I'd not see you in the first year of your life." He wanted to point out that she missed more than that, but didn't. "I told her that I never wanted to see her again if she was going to be like that. That she should...that she should just move away and not send me pictures or anything. Little did I know that all that would

165

come true."

"I'm sorry." He was too. Who knew what sort of person Grandma might have been if his mom hadn't been killed? "If you want to be my friend, I can do that. But I'm not going to go with you. I'm not going to be someone that jumps when you tell him to, either. And what you did to Roger? You should be ashamed of yourself. That man lost his wife and his baby, me. You treated him terribly, and that's not right either."

"I've blamed him all these years because he was the one that wanted to move out there. It was for his job, and he would have come home. He did come home after the year. But I broke him too, just like I did my daughter." Mel asked her about the other children. "He kindly, even after all I did to him, offered for me to be their grandmother, but I turned him down. They don't like me any more than you do."

"You really are a screw up, aren't you?" He didn't even regret the words after saying them. "Are you going to be able to live with yourself if anything happens to them? I mean, you lost your daughter with harsh words. What happens if you never get to know his kids? You have to remember, he lost as much if not more than you did, right? I'll tell you, you'll die a lonely old woman with no one to mourn your passing. Is that what you want?"

"You know, young man, no one talks to me like you are and gets away with it." He told her to go home then if she didn't like it. "You're very forward, aren't you? Well, I have to say...I have to tell you that I like that in you. Yes, you're right. I need to make up to them. I've been a bitter old woman, and I treated them poorly because of their father. And now he hates me too."

"Nah, I think he didn't like you before today." She told

him not to be sassy. "You need to take ahold of yourself and be nice. I'm not kidding. I thought for sure you were going to pull out a gun and make me come with you."

"Well, I might have, but I don't think we'd suit. We're much too much alike. But I do like you. I might even grow to love you. If you can keep that tongue behind your teeth." He said he wasn't even going to try. "Good for you. All right. I'm leaving, but expect me to come back. I want to know you, and I promise you, Mel, that I'll get on making up to the others too. And even to Roger. He's put up with a lot from me."

"I'm sure he has." She stood up and he did as well. "I'm glad that you understand why I can't go. And if you want to come by the greenhouse tomorrow, you'll see why I can't. I love my new job, and they like me there."

"And why wouldn't they? You're my grandson, after all." He hugged her too and walked her to the door. "You need anything? I mean, you seem to think you have it all."

"I do. And that's enough for me." She nodded and turned to leave, then looked at him again. "I'm fine. I promise you. You have things to do too. I'm just fine here."

Without another word she left him. And he had a feeling that it would be the last time he saw her too. She wouldn't come back for the simple reason that she'd not be able to make him do what she wanted and staying away would ensure to her that it was his fault, not hers. Whatever the reason, he was happy with the results of tonight.

Going to bed, he was sure he wasn't going to be able to sleep. But almost as soon as he laid his head on the pillow, Mel was out. Exhaustion was his best friend nowadays.

~~~

Dana saw the man while he and Sapphire were having

breakfast in town. Today was Wednesday, a big day for the restaurant since it was all you could eat pancakes. And seeing strangers in town stuck out like a sore thumb. He nodded in his direction when he entered where they were.

You think that's the man that Carmine was telling us about? He nodded and was glad that Sapphire was using their link. *I don't have time to mess with him today. I need to get over to Dragon's Breath. Let me know if we have to kill him.*

With that she kissed him on the mouth and laughed when he pulled her back for one more, this one a little more like he enjoyed them. As she went on her way, he stood up to go to the counter. Even for all you can eat, it was a cheap meal. Paying his ticket, he reached out to all of the dragons and told them what was going on.

You kept her home from school today, didn't you, Quinn? She said that she did when Danburn asked. *I'll warn Shawn and tell him what we think here. I don't want them going out there because they might think she's there and getting themselves killed.*

You're so sure that they'll be dead? Then Dana laughed. *Okay, you'd better tell him to make sure that the bodies are gone too.*

Dana noticed that there were a lot of out of county license plates around town, so perhaps he was just coming to the opening. They had put word out that it was opening today. Maybe that was all it was. But he didn't really believe his own words. Not with the way the man was dressed.

Suits weren't what one would wear to a grand opening. Nor did most people take a gun with them. He was armed, he could see that. And he wore dark glasses, like he didn't want anyone to know his face. He saw Mel walking to work and moved toward him to walk with him. Mel told him the car wouldn't start.

"You should get you a new one." He said he'd have to save up for it. that he didn't have any credit. "I'll co-sign for you. You need something more reliable."

"I know, but there is something about the old clunker that I like." They both laughed. "I will have something by winter, I promise. I can't be walking in the snow. I'll get sick again. I was sick one whole winter once. Pissed Melville off something terrible."

"You've made a decision to stop calling him Dad?" He told him about his visitors last night and what he'd said to them. "Good for you. I knew you had a good head on your shoulders. But you have to tell me, why is it that you don't think you'll see her anymore? I mean, didn't you say you parted on good terms?"

"I don't know. She's sort of set in her ways, I think. Anyway, I don't care. Not really and— Holy crap, look at all the people. Sapphire must be going about nuts right now."

Dana could feel her fear and told Mel to go on in, he'd deal with things out here.

All the carts were taken up by the people in the first part of the line. And there were small children riding in them. He was worried that it was going to be a stampede when the doors opened and didn't want anyone hurt. So he organized the people like he did his paints. Orderly and in straight lines.

At nine o'clock almost on the button, Denny and Mel came to the doors on the other side armed with maps of the place. He was glad for that—it might make things easier for them in their rush to get inside. As soon as the door opened, he watched as the two of them stood in front of the lines, another way to slow people down, and handed them a map with a general "*Hello*" and "*Welcome*" to each person. Sapphire was in the back, watching everything. He made his way back there.

"They were going to crush anyone that got in their way." He said he'd figured that out. "I was afraid that they'd kill each other. It's only a few flowers and shit. What is wrong with people?"

"I don't know, but you fixed it." She told him that Mel had. "Good for him. When Denny moves on to his next project, you going to put him in his place?"

"Yes, and I don't think, after today, that I'll have to convince him." Dana told her what he'd heard from Mel. "Good. I figured that she'd try and kidnap him or something to get him there where she could rule him. I have a feeling that her husband is going to see a difference in her too, if she holds to what she said she'd do."

"Hard to tell." She agreed. "The place looks really nice, Sapphire. You did a fantastic job. And all the other things you have, decorations for yards and stuff, that looks like something you'd see in the bigger stores."

"It was for a bigger store. And since I got it so cheap, free is cheap I think, I sort of passed the savings on to the people. Not half price, but I did double what I'd have to pay for it then took off twenty percent. That way if we have to order more, they won't be bitching about sticker shock." They walked around the place. She was dressed in jeans and a tee, not a company one, but she looked like she belonged here. When someone asked a question, she answered it and sent them on their way. This was going to be epic, he thought. "I have to go away for a few days. The sisters and I have a job."

"I wondered when you'd be going." She nodded but didn't look thrilled about leaving. "What is it, honey? You don't want to do this anymore?"

170

"I don't and I do. I love hiding the gems that we make. And knowing that someday people are going to find them and be so happy. Then there are times when I feel like what's the use. They make them perfect now, and why would anyone want one of my gems when they might have a small flaw in them?"

"I know what you mean. I was in a store once, a long time ago, and I saw what I thought was one of my pieces. It was made of plastic. I'd sold the piece to this man who in turn made copies of it to make a bit of cash off of my art. I was so pissed and depressed about that, it took me over a decade to get back to doing what I wanted."

The trees seemed to be a hot item. Some of them they'd gotten from the failed green house, and a lot of them were inventory that had been left there from the last time it had been a greenhouse. He saw two people arguing over which apple tree they wanted. Sapphire took out her marker and put ten percent off on them when they agreed to buy them both. He was laughing at her when she walked with him again.

"They were going to buy them anyway, but this way they think they took me. Why is it that people think they need to get a deal on everything? Or that they have to have a coupon when they go out to dinner? I buy what I want when I need it. I don't care if there is a sale. But if I come to buy, that's what I'm going to do."

"Not everyone has the funds to do that as we do." She told him she guessed that was it. "And humans as a whole like to think they've gotten the best deal possible on things. And so you understand, they didn't ask you for a discount. You gave it to them out of the kindness of your heart."

"Why do you have to be so nasty all the time?" He hugged

171

her to him. "I love this place, but now that it's running well, I'm ready to move onto something more. I was thinking about some of the shops in town. I don't want to run them, but I think I'd like to help them get going better. Inventory reductions, as well as marketing. For as long as I've been around, I can teach them a thing or two about selling."

"I'm sure you could easily, but talk to Kendrick. She has some ideas on some of the empty shops too. You two could go into business together. Even Cassie and Quinn could help you out. They're really good at this sort of thing too. See?"

They were both working the cash registers, having the best time ordering their husbands around while they bagged and wrapped purchases for them. And the line of people ready to check out was having fun too. It was a good way to keep tempers down while they had to wait, he thought.

"They insisted that they help. And Elissa is over there in the faerie garden area helping people purchase the things they'll need to get their own started. I wonder what they'd say if they knew that a real faerie lived in that little house, and is currently hanging around the flowers gathering nectar." Probably be impressed then freak out, Dana told her. "That's my thinking as well. Thank you for coming in to help out. I don't know what I would have done without you here."

"You would have done very well. And the fact that you really didn't need me should tell you that." She told him that she forever needed him. "And I you. Forever."

Chapter 11

Anthony Erickson moved in and out of the crowd like he was shopping for the perfect plant, when in reality he was looking for the child. The notes that he'd found when cleaning out the desk of his former employee, Ramon Packer, had given him enough information to know that she was going to bring him some good cash. But unlike his predecessor, he was looking for the girl all on his own, and had taken all the notes to his own little hiding place, then burned them when he had all that he could gather from them.

The girl was here. And the sooner he got her out of this little town, the better he'd be. Little towns knew every move you made. If you were a stranger in town, they watched you twice as hard. But today, this opening couldn't have come at a better time. There were a great many strangers in town.

There was also some babble about dragons in the notes that he'd found in Ramon's car when they'd released it to him. Dragons in this day and age? Not likely, but he was following up on every lead that he could find. And if there

173

were dragons here, then no one was talking about them.

He saw her about a second before she turned and looked at him. Standing next to a large man, holding her hand in his, Anthony wondered how he could lure her away. But almost as if she knew what he was doing, she whispered to the man and then took off toward the back of the shop. Anthony followed her and kept his eye on the man. There was no telling what she told him before leaving.

There were several port-o-johns lined up against the back of the large greenhouse, so he figured that was where she'd gone. He didn't want to look as if he were stalking someone, so he made sure to look at and pick up items before setting them back on the shelf. The man beside him asked if he was going to buy it, and it took him several seconds to realize he meant the plant and not the girl. Anthony handed it to him and walked away.

She came out of the third bathroom a few minutes later. But instead of going back with the man, she stood there and stared at him. Anthony had no idea why, but he felt his ass pucker tight and his balls curl up around his throat, it felt like. And when she walked toward him, Anthony looked around to see if this was a joke.

"You'll never get beyond the doors of this place if you try and take me." He showed her his gun. "That won't bother any of my family. You might just make them mad if you pull that out and think to use it."

"You're worth a great deal of money, and if I have to kill a couple of people to get what I want, then so be it. Why don't you come along with me nicely and no one has to get hurt?" She told him he would. "No, I won't. I've been doing this sort of thing for a very long time."

174

"Killing or taking little girls that aren't yours? I'm not going with you, Mr. Erickson." The fact that she knew his name startled him, but then he wasn't sure what the kid could do other than she could move things. "I can do a great many things that you don't know about."

"I'm assuming that you can read my mind too?" She nodded, and he knelt down to her level. "Little girl, you're going to come with me or I'll shoot this place up, and your parents too."

"All right, but like I told you, you won't get any further than the door before you're caught. And you might get out, but the dragons will take care of you when you do." He asked her what dragons. "That one is a dragon. That man over there, my dad, he's a dragon. And so is that lady in the green T-shirt. Most of the people working here, they're wolves. But they've been told to let the dragons handle you."

"They know that I'm here to get you?" She told him that she'd told them all. "Why not? I suppose that you have a connection to them all because they drank your blood. Or is it that you have a phone in the bathroom that you used?"

"No, silly. I have a cell phone with which I took your picture and sent it to them. They know who you are." He looked around and did notice that he was being watched by a great many of the people that she'd pointed out. "Are you sure you want to do this? You'll die if you do. And the dragons will make sure that no one ever knows that you were here today."

"That's murder." She only stared at him. "Look kid, come out with me and no one has to get hurt. You don't want me to shoot anyone, do you?"

"You won't get to." She was starting to get on his nerves.

175

This was a simple case of snatch and run. He had her right in his hands, and all he had to do now was run. But the door had never seemed so far away from him before. "Are you really thinking you can get away with this?"

He didn't, but he wasn't going to let some kid dictate to him what he could and couldn't do. Pulling her along behind him, he made it halfway there and no one had tried to stop him. He did notice that even the patrons of the place now seemed to be frozen in place, but he was nearly to the door now, and he was going to do it.

When a man rushed by him with a cart of flowers, he moved out of his way. When he did, Carmine pulled free of him and he turned in time to see that the dragons that she had pointed out to him were now gone. Just poof, they were not where they'd been before. He looked at the doorway now and felt the finger of fear take over.

"You still have time to change your mind." He didn't even look at her, but he did put out his hand and told her to take it. "I'm not allowed to go outside. They don't want me to see what they do to you."

"What is it they're planning to do?" When she didn't answer, he turned around to look at her. "What are they going to do to me, Carmine?"

"Nothing if you change your mind." He said that he wasn't going to do that. "They're going to kill you then. And not kindly either."

"What does that mean?" She shrugged, and he wasn't sure that not knowing was any better than if she had told him. His mind was a jumble of wolves tearing him apart and dragons burning him to a crisp and eating him. "Carmine, let's go. You and I can talk about your vivid imagination after we get away from here."

"I'm not leaving." She looked to his right and he was almost afraid to look there too. "The shoppers have no idea what is going on, Dad. So if you need to take care of him now, I don't care. He was going to sell me to someone. But they don't know about me yet. No one does but this man."

"So, if we take care of the threat now, we don't have to worry over it any more. No more looking over our shoulders." She nodded and then looked at him. The heavy hand on his shoulder made his bladder ache. "Mr. Erickson, you should know that the place is surrounded. If you leave here with the intent of taking my daughter, you'll never make it. We've already gotten rid of your car and contents."

"My car." Now what did he do? Pulling out his gun, he grabbed Carmine to him and put it to her head. "I want out of here, and you're going to allow me to have safe passage or I kill her."

"Carmine, did you know this?" She said that she didn't, but that was all right.

"He's not going to hurt you, is he?"

"No, Dad, he won't." Nodding, the man asked him again to leave his daughter alone. "He can't now, Dad. He's committed."

As he made his way to the door, he thought about the money that he might be getting. Right now, he thought there was a good chance he'd be lucky to get out alive. And when Carmine told him he wasn't going to, he wanted to pull the trigger and kill the fucking kid.

As soon as he was out of the building, he relaxed. But it was the wrong move. As soon as the gun slipped a little from her head, the child simply disappeared, and he felt himself lifted up. It wasn't until he was looking into the face of the ugliest creature he'd ever seen that he began to believe in dragons.

"Don't kill me, please? I won't tell anyone." The dragon didn't speak, but he did toss him through the air. When he landed in another dragon's palm, he knew a new kind of hell. This dragon was pissed, and he knew this was not going to end well.

"She wants me to tell you what she's saying." He looked at the man that had been trying to convince him not to leave. "Mr. Erickson, this is my wife, Quinn, sister to Carmine. And she wants me to tell you what she's saying."

"Can she talk?" He said not that he'd understand it. "Then how am I supposed to know what she's saying?"

"I'm going to tell you." He had said that, but in his fear, he'd forgotten. "She said to tell you that you should have a slow and painful death. But she doesn't have time for that today."

"Is she going to let me go until she has more time? I'm okay with that." The man laughed. "She's saying no, I take it."

"Quinn said that she might have made it a fast, quick death had you not put a gun to her sister's head. But that deserves some kind of punishment." His arm was ripped from his body and tossed away. Screaming, he almost missed what was said next. "And punishment from a dragon is not what you'd expect from anyone else."

His left leg was snapped off at the knee. Anthony was sick with the pain now, and he could see that she was enjoying herself. When she lifted her hand up, extended her claws out, he was sure that she was going to impale him, but all she did was eviscerate him. Anthony tried his best to hold his guts in with one hand while bleeding to death.

"Kill me now, please?" The big head shook, and he felt his leg break under the pressure of her claw. "Why are you doing this? I didn't get her—I didn't sell her to anyone. But do you know how much she's worth?"

"Everything to me." The giant claw touched his head, and he knew before she pushed it in that she was going to kill him this way. His brain was going to be smashed when she did—

~~~

Dana watched Sapphire. She'd been sitting on the swing on their deck since he'd brought her home. Carmine was in the house, taking a nap. She told him that she'd not slept well last night, knowing that anything could go wrong, and had worried.

"She'll be okay, won't she?" Dana had asked Carmine if she could read into her sister's future path. "No. Not yours either. It's like you're blocked. I could see just bits and pieces of it all, and that Quinn was going to make sure I was safe, but the rest, I didn't know."

Now she was safe, all of them were. He rocked back and forth on the rocker and decided to talk to Sapphire. Not about what happened today, but just talk. Dana decided to tell her about his piece.

"Faerie Home is finished as of today. And I've sold it. I was telling my agent that I've got it and he asked for some pictures. It was easy to do, just snap some with my phone and send them. What he should have told me was that he had a buyer, not for me, but another artist, in his office. The man wanted it badly, and I had to come up with an over inflated price because I wasn't sure that I wanted to sell it as yet.

Maybe never. But he didn't even haggle and bought Faerie Home without seeing it." She leaned back on his chest, but still said nothing. Dana continued to babble. "I have signed us up for a nice cruise. I think of all people, we deserve it. Also, Danburn has agreed to help the city with the installation of a new pool. It'll be finished about the time summer is over. But at least they have one for now. And Carmine can practice here as well as at home whenever she wants."

"She killed a man." He kissed her head and told her that it was fine. "No. It might have been had she just killed him, but Quinn made him suffer in the worst kind of way."

"He was going to sell off Carmine for the highest bidder. Now, since he'd never told a soul what he was about, no one else knows that she's here nor what she can do." Sapphire asked him if that made it all right. "Yes, to me it did. And to Quinn's dragon. Who did the killing, by the way. Quinn said that unlike Danburn's and mine, the dragon is like a separate being to her. She has conversations with her all the time. And when she tossed Anthony, she blacked out. Doesn't remember anything that happened until she was in the house after it was all over."

"Not her, but her dragon did that." She turned in his arms and looked at him. "Quinn never would have been able to do those things to him. And he did deserve it. He put a gun to the head of that little girl. So when the dragon took her mind and body, he made it so that she could live without any kind of memories of what she did. Quinn knows that he's dead, but nothing more."

They rocked for a little while longer, and just as the sun was hiding behind the trees at the back of their property, Sapphire spoke again.

"I'm going to stop doing the sapphires soon. I want to have children with you, and I don't think I'd be any good at gem dropping anymore anyway." He didn't ask her why, but she answered his unspoken question anyway. "I don't like humans. Not right now. I mean, today was good — fantastic — but I don't want them to have any joy in their lives by finding one of my sapphires. I want them to suffer in ways that I can't."

"You can't do that, honey." She asked him why not as she got up to pace. "Because it'll make you bitter and old before your time. Dragons are meant to bring joy to the world. It's the reason that we have so much magic, the reason that we were put here in the first place. We feed from the earth, and when the earth is happy, so are we. And vice versa."

"Are you saying that you want me to keep dropping gems? Because I will if you make me." He told her that it was doubtful that anyone could make her do what she didn't want to. "I just don't know what to do."

"Why does this bother you so much? I mean, it's not like you had anything at all to do with his death." She didn't answer him, so he persisted. "Carmine is fine. Quinn is all right with this too. So what is it — ?"

"I could have gladly done more to him for what he'd tried to do. Are you happy now? Your mate is a monster and could have killed that man without any kind of help from my dragon. I would have done more to his body while he lived, hurt him more, stripped him of his skin, his eyes. Then I would have taken out his black fucking heart and eaten it while he watched." He got up to go to her and she stopped him. "Don't touch me. I don't deserve to have you loving me."

He turned her around and jerked her body flush against

181

his. "I would have done worse too. Could have, because when he was tossed to her, I could easily have caught him up and taken him away to use my human self to hurt him. Cut him to ribbons before I burned him alive. You don't think that any one of us would have loved to have had the chance?" He shook her when she didn't answer. "That dragon saved us all from having to live with ourselves after he was dead. Not even Quinn, who was the one that actually did it, can remember what his face looked like when she jerked his arm from the socket. Not a clue that he begged her over and over to end his life."

He held her while she sobbed, and when he heard the tink-tink of something hitting the deck beneath them, he looked down at the tears of a dragon and what she was producing.

"I'm so sorry." He told her to look at the gems. "I don't care about the gems right now. I pissed you off, and I ache with that."

"Sapphire, your gems are diamonds and sapphires." She looked at him with a crystal forming on her cheek. Taking it away with his thumb, he watched as it formed a perfect sphere of a diamond and sapphire right before his eyes. "This is beautiful. I mean, it's like it took both of us to make something so unique that people might start looking for the gems again."

"You think this is going to be a norm for us?" He said that he didn't know, but she should look at the ones at her feet. When she stepped back, he knelt down and looked at them. "They're all spheres. Like they were formed to be something beautiful right away."

On some of the balls the diamond was part of the sphere. One of them had a vein of it right through the middle, while several more had them snaking through them like a river along a beautiful water. There was one that he was keeping. The diamond was more than half the sphere, and the sapphire looked like a waterfall coming down off of a snowy mountain. The imperfections of the sapphire made it feel like you could almost touch the water and be wet from it.

There were about a dozen in all, not counting the one that he was keeping. And Sapphire found one that was exactly like his but for the gems being reversed. He loved them both very much. And more so because Sapphire had made them for him.

"Do you think this is what I'm going to be making for the drops?" Her voice was low and in awe, and he knew just how she felt. He asked her to make one, just to be sure. And as soon as one tear landed on her cheek, he knew that she was making them from now on.

"I'm going to make this one into a water design. And have it so that the ball will forever be turning in it. It'll be all ours, this gem. The first of many that will be found soon, I guess."

"Not soon. Not yet. We have to tell the sisters. For all we know, they could be producing these as well." He didn't think so, but he'd not thought this was possible. "They're perfect, aren't they? People will think them fake. And while some are as big as that one, softball sized, there are ones small enough to be put into a setting for a lovely ring."

"Yes, I know. I think that they're the most beautiful gems I've ever seen. But for my gem, you." He laughed when she stuck her tongue out at him. "Such a romantic you are."

Gathering them up, she heard from the sisters. No, they didn't produce them solely, but they did have one or two of them in their drop. To think that these ladies had somehow

183

saved themselves from being pushed out of work by man-made products.

They brought over their work and he marveled that the ones with diamonds in them were all spheres, while the ones that they produced that were uniquely their own were rough stones that would need to be cut and polished before being used.

The girls tried several more times to make more, but all they got for their efforts was one each time. None of them but Opal. She could take her tear and mix it with one of the others, and it would grow into a large rough stone. The rest couldn't do that.

"So you can make opal diamonds, rubies, and emeralds. And so you know, I'm taking one each of them. I want to put them up as the first ever." They all agreed that he could have them. Dana wasn't sure what he'd have done had they said no. But they told him that they loved him and that was fine by them. He'd not tell them, but he loved the combination of the opal and diamond. It was by far the prettiest of them all.

The tears, just regular tears, would take a little of their DNA as they traveled down their cheeks and dropped. Once they had whatever else they needed, he wasn't entirely sure, but once they were formed with the needed ingredients, they would form as they fell. Sometimes they would continue to form on the ground, taking on the DNA of the earth below it. that would be the imperfections that would be found in the gems. And if it landed on something, a flower or some water, you'd get a quite different piece that would be marveled over for decades. Like the Hope Diamond.

It was blue in color because at some point he must have stumbled upon a bit of Sapphire to turn it that color. There was no shifting of the gems then, but a single bit of her and him making a diamond had formed the largest gem he'd ever made. And instead of keeping it, which he supposed he could have, he left it to be found by some human who might need it. It was still around, he marveled at that, and had gone to see it once.

When the girls—as he had begun to think of them as just girls—agreed to stay for dinner, they all had a wonderful time around the big table. There were things that they were still working out. They lived in their own houses now and seemed to be enjoying the quiet when they got it. But more often than not, they'd end up in one of the three houses and invite young Mel over. He was becoming good friends with them all.

"You think that it would be rude of me to ask him to move in with us?" Dana asked if he was one of their mates. "No, nothing like that. He's like a little brother to us, and we want to keep him around. He's really good at moving big boxes and stuff."

"You have magic for that. And don't do it, please?" They asked Sapphire why not. "Because he's saving for his own home. The one he's in now. And if he moves in with you three, even for a little while, you'll make him forget his dreams. He's a good human and needs to feel like he's something."

"I can see that. He does take a lot of pride in his home. Did you know that he takes home the broken plants and brings them back most of the time? We help them out when we see them, but he's getting to have himself a showcase at his place. And an apple tree as well as a plum. My two favorite fruits." Sapphire told Opal that they were all her favorites. "Okay, you're right about that. But you're right, we won't ask him."

They ended up staying the night. Dana liked having them

there. They were his girls, even though he looked to be about the same age as them. But they were his girls, and he was going to make sure that they were just fine.

Chapter 12

Griffith wasn't ready for a mate. He had a feeling that no matter how many times he said that, she'd show up at the worst time. The house he'd purchased was coming along nicely, thanks in part to the sisters. They had taken to dropping off their purchases to him in the last week, and he had a feeling that it would have to do with his mate. Not even asking Carmine would get him any answers.

"She'll come when she does." He said that he knew that. "Well, then why are you asking me? I'm just a kid."

"Honey, you are not even close to be just an *anything*. Especially not just a kid. But if you divine something, let me know. All right?" She said that she would, but she had a smile on that he didn't think boded well for him. "You will, right?"

"I said that I would."

He had bothered her too much. When she was doing her homework, he was supposed to come back later. But this was important to him. He didn't want his mate to come up on him when he was least expecting it. He thought of his brother and shivered.

"She does not need that in her life."

Griffith sat down now on his deck and watched the animals come out to play in the early morning sun. It was late enough in the summer where there were all kinds of things lurking about. And his favorite creatures were the brownies that came up on the deck to talk to him.

"Did you find out anything?" He told Bud that he'd not. "Too bad. Are you going to share that watermelon? Or eat it all for yourself? You're starting to be a little pudgy around the middle, Griffith. I'd watch the sweets if I were you."

"I'm not fat, tubby." He loved the way that the brownies would talk about their bellies like they were children. They took a great deal of pride from having the biggest one. Of course, it interfered with their work at times, being too fat to fly, but they enjoyed life too much to let it get to them. "I was wondering if you have any more of those seeds you gave me the other week. I don't know what you did to them, but I have the prettiest vines hanging all off the roof of the porch."

"I gave it a little loving. You should try it." He didn't even want to hazard a guess as to what that might mean, so just asked for the seeds. "I have some, but you must let me come and gather the new seeds up when you've done with the plants of the year. Those are pretty, and I've been putting them on old houses for about fifty years now. Makes them look less decrepit."

"I thought that the flowers looked familiar. I want to plant these on the sunny side of the barn. They'll be all right there, don't you think?" He said that they liked the sun. "I'm going to build a trellis next spring to put out over the steps to the porch."

"Sounds like a right fine idea, that. Hey, you think that lady gardener, she'd let us come and have her leftovers at the end of the season? We can trade off what we have, and she'll have the best plants ever." He said that he'd ask her. He reached out to Sapphire then or he'd forget, and Bud would annoy him until he did.

I can do that but ask him if I can hire a couple of dozen of his kind to come and help me with the new seeds. I don't know anything much about brownies. He asked Bud and his chest puffed out. *I don't even know how to pay a brownie.*

Sweets. They love them, and it helps them have more energy. But not candy if you can help it. They eat too much of that as it is. Just sweet fruit and tomatoes. They love tomatoes. He asked Bud what his opinion was. *He said that he'd be happy to help you, and to find you a good crew. For that, he said he'd give you one hundred different seeds. Some of them are all but gone now from the humans.*

You mean heirloom seeds? That'll be fantastic. Tell him I said thanks a bunch.

He told Bud that he'd made the sapphire dragon very happy.

"What are you planning to do now? You got yourself something to do all day, or you going to be a lazy bum and sit on your brain?" He told Bud that he was planning to do just that. "No, you're not. You're much too smart for that. Why don't you come on down to our factory and help us out?"

"You have a factory?" He told him that everyone had to have someplace that made goods. "Yes, I suppose. What sort of things do you make?"

"We have a place now that just makes chairs. The sapphire dragon, she gave us a bunch of soft wool that we're making into covers for chairs. They're so soft on the butt. I was wondering if you could come and bring that noisy cutter thing that I heard you using, and cut us some little branches off with it." It took him a moment to realize that he meant the chain saw. "That's the contraption. You bring it with you and I'll set you to work. And we'll take care that your house is all spit and polished too."

"You mean clean up after me?" He told him what he meant. "I would enjoy that. You guys making sure that the bushes are all right and trimmed. Also, the trees, I guess."

"Whatever needs attention, we can do it. You'll see." He knew that he would too. His lawn was too big for him to take care of on his own, if he was inclined to do so. And the trees were dropping more and more branches all the time. He wondered what he was going to do about that. "You can bring us some of them flowers that the sapphire dragon sells, and we'll pretty them right up too."

"Her name is Sapphire. Why do you call her the sapphire dragon, like it's a title or something?" He said it was a title to him. "I guess so. She and her sisters are going to be gone for a week starting tomorrow. They call it dropping their gems. Did you hear about the new ones that they're able to make?"

"I seen it myself or I'd of not believed it. Nearly didn't want to believe something so pretty could be coming from a tear, though. I wonder at the hurt one would have to be able to cry when they need to." He told him how it worked. "You're joshing me. Really, you can just ask for them and the tears form?"

"Yes. While I make any kind of gem, it does depend on my mood as to what I get. Green is from a pleasant mood. Rubies are for when I'm angry. And then there are the ones that I cry for just the sake of needing money. That will be about anything." Bud said he could see that. "But with the sisters four, Opal, Sapphire, Emerald, and Ruby, they were created to make the gems for the human population. It was to try and keep them from taking a dragon back in the day."

"I heard that one too. I didn't know if I believed it or not, but I heard it." Bud sat down on a chair that he told him he'd brought from home. "Sure would be nice to have us some help on those chairs. They're going to put them in the shop, I heard."

"I'd not heard that." He was teasing the little guy and stood up to go and get his clippers and chainsaw. Whatever they needed done, he was willing to help. Bud had been his companion a great deal over the last few weeks.

Gathering up his gloves too, he headed out to the field he was sure that either he owned or one of the others did. As soon as he was ready to start the chainsaw, however, he had them take cover. It was too loud for his ears; he couldn't imagine what it would sound like to them.

After cutting down the tree that he'd been told was safe, he began cutting the smaller branches off and putting them in piles. There were different kinds they needed, he knew. Green would bend well, and the darker ones that were already dry would make the best legs and seat bottoms. Almost as soon as he had the tree dismantled to what they could use, a large pip of faeries came and took away all the shavings. He knew they were going to use that for mulch for the newer plants.

At lunch time he went home to get himself a much needed sandwich. He had to admit, he felt better just getting out and doing something. He'd been down for too long, and it had affected him. Now that he was out in the sun and having some fun, he was willing to bet that Bud had known that, and

191

took them all back some of the cookies that he'd gotten from Cassie last night.

"We need a bit of a fire." Griffith asked Bud why. "Well, we have to make sure that the sugar doesn't come out on the chairs and onto our floors."

He could see that, but the grass was terribly dry. "Does it have to be done now? I mean, can we wait until after a bit of rain? I don't want to burn down the forest, and it might happen with all this dry grass."

Bud looked around and flew to the trees. He was asking their opinion, he knew that, and started out to find them a similar tree like they had before. When Bud returned he asked about the tree, then the fire.

"We're going to wait, as you said. The trees, they said that they're much too brittle now and it would hurt them." He said that was smart of him to ask the trees. "Thank you for reminding me that we're not the only ones in the forest."

"My pleasure."

They worked until supper time. They were planning a big day for working tomorrow now that they had enough wood. He never thought about how they got a tree down to use, and they said that they'd have to gather them all up, drag them to where they were working, and then take them apart. It would slow them down for a week just to get ready to make them.

On his way home, he picked up a few of the flowers that were in the field. He'd not destroy them, but would enjoy them for a while then plant them back in the soil for the next person to see. When he was ready to make his own dinner, Bud joined him again.

"We got some information for you." He nodded as he fired up the grill to make himself some steaks. "The woman that is coming for you, she's close. Like in the mountain close."

Griffith nearly burned his hand off when he stared at him for too long. "In the mountain or on the mountain? And why is she there and not in one of the houses here in town?"

"Your brother." His heart started to pound when he heard that James was close. "He spotted her a few days ago and has hurt her."

"James is that close as well?" He said that he didn't know it was him until today. "And why are you telling me this? I thought that there was some kind of rule about giving away too much information."

"You helped us. We wanted to return the favor." He nodded and pulled his steaks off the grill, no longer hungry. "She is hurt, but on the mend. I don't know that James did it or not, but she's sewed herself right together and is resting inside the cave."

"Do I need to go and get her?" He said that he'd not. "Why not? I mean, you said she's my mate. I don't want her out there when I could be caring for her."

"You look too much like him." He sat down, the dinner now forgotten on the platter by the grill. "You'll scare her should you go up there. And she's armed with magic."

"What is she?" He said that the earth said she was of it, the soil. "That could mean just about anything. Can you give me more than that? Can you go and —?"

Bud took off and he nearly ran after him when he realized he'd never catch him. When he returned, he looked upset.

"You need to be your dragon. Now." Not even waiting to find out what was going on, he shifted to his beast. "Come with me and I'll show you. I wasn't aware that your brother cannot shift."

"My mother was dragon, my father human. They created one dragon and one human when they had us. We're twins." Bud said that he knew that now. "What's happened, Bud? Is she hurt?"

"Yes." They entered the cave, which was just big enough for him to get into. But it narrowed as he made his way down. And it was then that he could hear her screams for help. Shifting so that he could move faster, Griffith followed the voice until he came to a cliff, where she was hanging from it for dear life.

"Not you. Go the fuck away." He said he wasn't James. "How stupid do you think I am? Of course you are."

"I'm Griffith, and I'm not going to hurt you." He reached for her arm and when he touched her, she screamed in pain. He nearly let her go but pulled her up and laid her gently on the ground. "What happened?"

"I was just skipping along, minding my own business, when this giant hole just jumped up in front of me." He nearly laughed at her tone. "I fell, you fucking moron. You have to be related to James—he never gets my sarcasm."

"Oh, I got it all right. I just thought laughing at you would get me hurt." She just glared at him. "I'm a dragon. And I'm going to start a small fire so I can have a look at you before I move you, all right?"

The fire blazed for a moment before settling down. He sent Bud to get more wood, and when he returned with some, Griffith put one of the dryer sticks in to use as a flashlight. She was really scraped up but seemed to be all right. That was until she turned her arm around where he could see the back of it.

"Christ, that's why you screamed." She just glared at him.

"I'm sorry, but are you always like this? Or is it the pain that makes you sort of cranky?"

"You said that you were related to James, so you know what sort of person he is." He said that he was sorry for anything that he'd done. "Yeah, well, that doesn't heal me like I want. He's a mean jerk off."

"I'm truly sorry." She nodded and he picked her up. "I'm going to take us to my house and get you some help, all right?"

"Flying?" He said if it was all right with her. "You're different than he is. Or is this for my benefit? I know what you are to me, pecker head, so don't be kind because you think you're going to get laid. You're not."

"Man, and here I thought I had an easy woman." He stood up and told her to hang on. When he was out of the tunnel enough, he let his dragon take him as he held onto their mate. Halfway home, he saw James in his driveway. "I'm taking you to the back of the house. Bud will let you in. Just be quiet while I deal with him."

~~~

James fucking hated his brother. This house was another prime example of the shit that he got when James had gotten nothing. Of course, he'd been left the family estate, but that only went so far when he had to keep paying off women he'd hurt. But he loved to hurt people too much to quit now.

"James. What are you doing here?" He turned when he heard his brother's voice and looked him over. As usual, he looked picture perfect and in good shape. It made him realize how fat he'd gotten over the years and tried sucking in his gut. "What are you doing here, I asked you."

"Can't a man come and see his little brother?" Griffith told him he was only older than him by several minutes. "Well, that makes me the eldest. I came to tell you that I've sold the family castle. To an unknown— You bought it, didn't you? Mother fuck, is there nothing I can do without you sticking your nose in it?"

"I have no idea. But yes, I bought the castle back from the bank. But you can't go there to live. You've got enough money to start up someplace else, and I suggest you get on with it. Not around here. I have my life just the way I like it, and I don't want you here fucking it up." He told him he'd found his mate. "Really? And who, pray tell, is stupid enough to want to be shackled to you for the rest of her short life?"

"She's a faerie. A pretty redhead." Still he said nothing. "I've misplaced her. I was hoping that you could use your considerable skills that I didn't get, even though I'm the oldest, and fly around and find her for me."

"How can you misplace a mate? Or is it that you want me to believe that she's your mate? And no, I'm not going to help you get her back. She's gone, and that's good for her. You hurt her very much before she ran?" He smiled. "Believe it or not, I don't think you're very charming to people, no matter what sort of face you put on."

"You've always had it all, haven't you, Griff? Even now you own the house that I was left, probably have tons of money and diamonds and shit stashed all over the house. Just give me some and I'll be on my way. It's the least you can do for me." He told him not giving him anything was the least he could do, and that's what he was going to do. "Come on, damn it. Get me some jewels and my mate, and I'll not bother you again for a while."

"You mean until the money runs out? Or till you're in trouble again, James? You seemed to be a magnet to trouble.

Most of it you cause yourself." A car pulled in the drive and he saw it was Griff's friend, Kip. He hated him as much as he did Damn-bird. Fuckers all of them. "You remember my brother, don't you, Kip? He's here to beg money off me. Oh, and he found his mate, but she's run off."

"She didn't exactly run off so much as she broke free. You know how I like my sex, brother dear. And she didn't care for it that rough."

"No one likes it like you do, James. And most of the time, if I remember correctly, you would murder them when you finished with them. That caused a great deal of heartache around the town. You're not welcome here." James hated to be told no almost as much as he hated his brother and his buddies. "Go away and find her if you can. I don't care."

They went into the house, and he had no choice but to go back to his car. Griff would have some sort of spell on his home that would prevent him from coming inside. And it usually came with a bit of pain when he tried. As he drove out of the drive, he looked in the wooded area for the girl. Once he found her, he was going to throw her into that fucking cave he'd found her in. The insolent bitch.

By nightfall he'd not found her. He knew that she was hurt—he'd made sure to mark her before he tied her to the tree. To have had her, naked and ready for him, he was getting hard just thinking about her. As soon as he found her, he was going to fuck her in every orifice that she had. And then come all over the bitch before getting rid of her body.

James had about a thousand bucks to his name. When the bank had sold the castle off, he thought he'd get most of that money. But he'd had to pay whatever closing costs were, as well as pay the back taxes on the house. It came out to exactly enough to pay it off and give him the thousand he now had. He just knew that Griff had done that to him.

"It'll have to do me, I guess."

He wasn't dumb enough to go out and spend his money stupidly. He'd not buy a new suit or go to a fancy hotel and live it up. He had to be frugal and not be broke by the end of the day. Going to the grocery store in this little town, he bought himself noodles in those plastic containers that had seasoning in them, some bottled waters, and a box of cereal. The gallon of milk that he wanted but had nowhere to store turned into a quart. One thing that he did love was ice cold milk.

Maybe he'd find the girl and sell her off to some of the people he knew that liked it like he didpreferences. Hard and rough, like he was mining for gold when he fucked a woman. And when he came, it was like his entire body came with his cock. He was the best at violent sex that he knew, and women knew too.

He'd always had a taste for the violent things in life. Twice when they were younger, James had tried to kill Griff. For some reason he thought that if he killed Griff and was close enough, his dragon would come to him.

When he'd asked his dad about it, he told him that it didn't work that way, and told him he was appalled at his behavior. His father was the first person in a long line of people that he'd killed. Slicing his head from his body had been much easier than he'd thought it should have been. That's when he found out that not only did he have superhuman strength, but he also liked the feel of blood on his face and chest.

From then on, if someone pissed him off or told him no, he would kill them. The only two people that he wasn't able to kill was his mother and his brother. Neither of them would die like he wanted them to.

Then he'd found out about iron in the system of a dragon. His mother had been dead within a week. And who knew that their body would disappear like she had? He'd gone up to her room to feed her more of the nasty shit, and she had vanished. Manfred, the house servant, had told him that she was gone, that her body had left this world.

Then just a few days later, he'd noticed that all the staff had disappeared too, in a puff of smoke. And they robbed him before they left. He supposed that robbing wasn't what it really was, since he'd not paid them in months. But they were gone, and he was there all alone, until he realized that he could bring his *dates* there. After that, it was a good old time had by him.

"Now my mate is missing." He knew that she wasn't his mate, but sometimes bitches would put out more easily if they thought they had found their other half. And for him, cooperation was nice but not necessary. And he liked them to be uncooperative to a point, like when he was fucking them.

He had to find a place to sleep, so he drove his car to the abandoned hotel that was out on Route Forty and pulled his car around back. The bank was looking for the car and he needed it at the moment. As soon as he got inside the place, he knew why someone had let it go. It was a fucking mess. But he didn't care about that so long as there were no rats in his bed and he had a roof over his head. Finding the one room that had that, the front office, was difficult, but he finally had a place to lay his head. Tomorrow he'd find the woman and teach her the meaning of staying still.

"Yes, ma'am, you're going to learn the hard way how I

199

like things done." Closing his eyes, he let sleep take him.

Before You Go...

HELP AN AUTHOR

write a review

THANK YOU!

Share your voice and help guide other readers to these wonderful books. Even if it's only a line or two your reviews help readers discover the author's books so they can continue creating stories that you'll love. Login to your favorite retailer and leave a review. Thank you.

AWARD WINNING, BESTSELLING AUTHOR

Kathi Barton, winner of the Pinnacle Book Achievement award as well as a best-selling author on Amazon and All Romance books, lives in Nashport, Ohio with her husband Paul. When not creating new worlds and romance, Kathi and her husband enjoy camping and going to auctions. She can also be seen at county fairs with her husband who is an artist and potter.

Her muse, a cross between Jimmy Stewart and Hugh Jackman, brings her stories to life for her readers in a way that has them coming back time and again for more. Her favorite genre is paranormal romance with a great deal of spice. You can visit Kathi online and drop her an email if you'd like. She loves hearing from her fans. aaronskiss@gmail.com.

Follow Kathi on her blog: http://kathisbartonauthor.blogspot.com/